The District Detectives

The Silence Broken: Part 1

Janelle Arens

ISBN: 1544894023
ISBN-13: 978-1544894027

To: Crystal

The girl who dragged me through the pages of history and showed me a class of men that will not soon be forgotten, in a way no teacher ever could.
For introducing me to the detective that is Dick Tracy, and because we've always wanted a detective who wouldn't be stopped by a locked door.

Nicole,

You're one of the best
work buddies ever!
Welcome to Big Town and
happy reading!

♡ always,

Janelle Evans

3/7/2017

Chapter 1

Early 1920s.
Big Town USA's Warehouse District.
Joey Leftfoot's headquarters.

The big black sedan rolled up, and its brakes complained the car to a squeaky stop in front of an old, dilapidated-looking warehouse. The driver quickly sprang from his seat and grabbed the back door handle. He stepped back and stood at attention with the door in front of him.

First a left foot encased in an expensive leather shoe stepped out and landed on the pavement. The man the shoe belonged to swung up and out of the car. He stood to his full height--well over six feet--his right hand swinging a thin, light brown leather strap over his shoulder. The menacing nose of a Tommy gun swung into position between his arm and his body, nose toward the ground. He surveyed the building and frowned. "Not quite the same as the New York boys," he sniffed to his driver in a smooth baritone.

"Not quite, Ace." The driver calmly agreed with him.

"Well, let's see what these small-timers have for me." Ace started away and then stepped back and leaned closer to his driver. "Oh, Wheels, if you hear shooting. Start the car."

"Sure thing," Wheels answered around the cigarette that was clamped between his lips. He leaned against the driver's door and pulled a match out of the inner pocket of his coat. He leaned to his right a little and dragged the match head across the spare tire's hubcap, which rode in the running board just in front of the driver's door.

Ace marched right up to the door that looked like it could fall off its hinges. He jerked the door open and without a backwards glance at Wheels, breezed into the building.

Some lower-level thugs were in the hallway that Ace walked through, but they only gave him a quick glance. His expensive suit and broad shoulders were enough to convince most of them that they were better off leaving him alone. For the men who weren't as easily convinced, a good look at the coffee brown eyes that were shaded under the black fedora and the nose of the Tommy gun that poked out between his right arm and his body was more than enough to let them know that he was the type of man that wouldn't cringe away from shooting first and asking questions later...if ever.

Ace walked right up to the door that he knew would lead into the office. He brushed past the protesting guard and burst into the room without knocking. "Gentlemen, I'm here," he announced to the men in the room.

The burly man who was lining up a shot on the pool table looked up at him with the look of someone who was used to running a tight ship and not being barged in on. "You must be the gunman from the east," he greeted, not looking amused.

Ace ignored the look. He bowed slightly, his eyes never leaving the men in the room. "You called. Joey Leftfoot, I presume."

The man at the pool table stood up and eyed the newcomer for a moment. After Joey seemed satisfied with what he saw, he nodded and went back to his shot. "I hear that you're quite the Ace in the deck." He looked at his two companions. "These are my men. Razor," Joey nodded to a man who looked to be much younger than the rest of them. He too had a cue, an expensive suit, and his black hair was slicked back. His dark eyes didn't look like they missed anything, and Ace was right in assuming that he was smart, to the point of conniving. "And Two-Timer." Two-Timer looked to be about the same age as Joey; he had the smile of a fox.

"Looks about as slippery as a fish,"

Ace muttered. One look at the thin man disgusted him.

"I like to think so." Two-Timer walked over to the small bar and poured himself a scotch. When he turned around his pale eyes were calculating. "Nice of you to make the trip so quickly."

"We have a bit of a problem," Joey picked up. "There's a man in town that's been a thorn in my side for quite some time." His eyes narrowed when Razor knocked two balls into a pocket.

Razor cleared his throat. "He's a detective."

"You couldn't take care of a detective yourselves?" Ace scorned. "It's just a badge."

Razor glanced at Joey. "He's not just *any* badge. We haven't shaken him yet. He's very tenacious."

Two-Timer cleared his throat. "You'll have to forgive the respectful tone in Razor's voice. It has become apparent that he thinks that Wainwright is good at what he does." Two-Timer sneered at Razor.

Razor stared back. "It's prudent to respect your enemies. Especially the ones that are good at what they do. That way you'll never underestimate them and be taken by surprise," he pointed out calmly, lining up his next shot.

Ace's eyebrows rose. He looked at Joey. "So I'm here to rub this Wainwright out."

Joey shook his head. "Just rattle him enough to shake him off my trail for a

4

while." He shot the cue ball toward the other end of the table with surprising force.

"Dead men can't follow a trail," Ace came back.

"Wainwright stays alive!" Joey snarled at the challenge. "I have other plans for him." He was *not* about to be challenged by a gunman, especially a new one from the East.

Ace shrugged. "Make too many plans and one's sure to backfire." He suddenly found himself with the skinny end of the pool cue pressed tightly against his throat. Joey was looking him square in the eye.

Joey still looked pleasant, but his voice was hard and cold. "You're on *my* turf now. You will do as *I* say. Or those boys back East that are wondering where you dropped off the map will know exactly where you are. Clear?" Joey advanced, pushing Ace back with his cue until the hitman's back bumped into the wall. Joey's hand slid up the pool cue and he pulled the handgun out of Ace's sleeve and held it up in front of the hitman's eyes, with an almost menacing look on his face.

Ace narrowed his eyes for a second. He didn't like the fact that Joey had just taken a gun out of his possession, but when the cue pressed tighter against his throat, he nodded. "Crystal," his voice was slightly scratchy because force on his vocal cords.

"Good. I'm glad to hear it," Joey

nodded, his voice civil once again. He held out the handgun for Ace to take and walked back to the pool table, quickly shooting two solid balls into a corner pocket. "Two-Timer will take you to your quarters." There was a perfectly round red chalk mark on Ace's throat where the cue had been.

Ace looked Two-Timer over again and then nodded. "Thank you, Joey."

Joey smiled broadly. "It's my pleasure. Welcome to Big Town, Ace." He turned his back in dismissal, and the two men left the room eyeing each other. The heavy door thudded closed.

Two-Timer waited until they were around the corner so the guard outside the door wouldn't hear them. He looked over at Ace. "Makes you want to kill him when he makes a fool out of you like that, doesn't it?" he asked, his voice slick.

Ace looked at him contempt in his coffee eyes.

Two-Timer didn't seem to notice the look. He leaned closer. "If you do ever decide to get Joey back, I'll handle the logistics."

Ace glared at him. "If I kill him, I do it alone. I don't do business with snakes."

Two-Timer's eyes flashed for a moment, and then his smug look returned. "Keep it in mind."

"I take it Ace knows that you have connections back east," Razor said to the room as he lined up a shot on the pool table.

Joey leaned on his stick and chuckled. "Probably. But he's a straight enough shot that he's worth a death threat. Not that those boys would send anyone this way to back up their words. Their hands are too full at the moment."

"I certainly hope that's the way of it, Joey." Razor nodded, indicating that it was Joey's turn.

Razor was sitting in a speakeasy weeks later when Ace bulled in through the door, his three gun dogs tumbling in behind him. Something about the way that he was smiling warned Razor that the burly goon had killed someone. "Take a seat, Ace. No one's sitting there," Razor intoned in a pleasant voice over the lip of his moonshine glass as Ace threw himself down in the chair across from Razor.

Ace narrowed his eyes at the obviously rude invite. "You're lucky I'm in a good mood, Kid," he snarled.

Razor leaned forward and looked around the room like he was telling a secret. "Don't tell anyone else, they might not know what to do with it," he warned, looking concerned that someone else might find out. His eyes slid over his right shoulder when there was a ruckus on the small stage in the back corner. The band had been arguing about something but soon broke out into a lively swing tune.

"If you weren't Joey's pet, you'd be

dead." Ace glared at him.

"I'm aware." Razor sat straight again. He took a sip of the moonshine and regarded Ace over the rim. "Did you and your boys have fun shooting up town today?" he wondered, his voice bored.

A rare smile flashed across Ace's face. "It's done. Wainwright won't be following anyone for a while."

Razor set down his glass on the table. "You sound positively overjoyed. You didn't use him for target practice, did you?" his voice hardened.

Ace didn't seem to hear Razor's jab, or he was too in the moment to care. "No. I didn't kill him, I certainly left something for him to remember though. Weeks of causing trouble and waiting for the perfect moment. The chance came today."

Razor looked at him, and for the first time, he narrowed his eyes. "What did you do you trigger-happy bull?" he demanded.

Ace's face pulled back into a wicked smile. "Took the chance given to me."

Ten years later…

The hand-drawn sketch was the first paper in the well-worn, dilapidated file. Ace's face was turned a quarter-turn from forward, his eyes were narrowed, and his lips were pressed tightly together. His jaw muscles were clenched and he couldn't be mistaken for anything but deadly. The corners of the paper were dog-eared and the paper itself looked like it had been handled quite a bit. The next sheet of paper was a compilation of information on where he was born, supposedly; where he grew up, according to speculation; and when he got his start in the world of organized crime at about fifteen—that date known well. The next three pages were overflowing with his rap sheet; both the known offences, and the crimes that pointed to him but hadn't been proved.

This file had been missing from its appropriate place in the library in Wainwright Detective Agency for years. It was well-used by only one person. It was in a desk drawer, constantly inches from finger tips that knew exactly how to pull it out without the help of searching eyes. She was obsessed with getting to know him better than anyone else so she could bring him to justice. Her grey-green eyes would stare at the picture, like they were now, memorizing every detail for the thousandth time. She could recite—verbatim—the statistics and rap sheet without looking, almost better than her home address. When the file was out, it was just herself and the file of the man she hated.
"…Olli…Olli…Olivia Wainwright!"

Olli blinked and looked over the edge of the file at a holographic image of a girl about the same age as she was. "Hm?"

"Put that file away. You have more important things to do," the image told her, an almost harsh tone edging her voice.

Olli looked at her for a moment and then went back to studying the picture. "I beg to differ."

"Olli, you're not going to get *anything* done by just looking at a drawn picture of the man," the image pointed out.

Olli closed the file, her thumb still in it for quick opening. "See, that's the difference between you and me, Dee. I happen to think that it helps."

"How? You know that file better than your office, Olli. It's not like you're going to learn anything new from it."

Olli opened it again. She looked up when Dee sighed and shrugged. "You never know."

"Olli, it doesn't help you to obsess about something that you can't change. It's in the past. *Ten* years ago."

Olli's jaw hardened. "I can make sure that it doesn't happen again."

Dee folded her arms and raised her eyebrows. "How? By pouring over an old file that you know by heart while ignoring the mess that is your office?"

Olli closed the file and slipped it into its drawer. "How do you expect to motivate me to do anything if you use that motherly tone and look? You know you're not my mother."

Dee tilted her head to the left and sighed. She uncrossed her arms and folded her hands behind her back. "If I were your mother, I would say something along the lines of: Must you wear that?"

Dee's right hand motioned to Olli as a whole.

Olli looked down at what she was wearing. "What's wrong with what I'm wearing?" she asked, a slight defensive note edging into her voice.

Dee's eyes flared open and her hands turned palm up toward the ceiling. "You really don't know?" She sighed and folded her hands. "Well, let's start with your blouse."

"What's wrong with it?" Olli protested.

"It's grey, for starters. Dull, boring, blend-into-rock, grey," Dee started.

"But-" Olli interjected.

"And look at those sleeves, Olli! They're baggy and droopy. Your arms look positively fat," Dee continued like she hadn't heard Olli.

Olli frowned and picked up her right arm. Her dark dove grey blouse sleeve billowed slightly with her movement. "I need them to be wide. I need the arm movement."

"You never wear bright colors. Always dark blues and greys of every color, but light greys, and *black*! Why can't you wear yellows, and greens, and reds? You look so beautiful in yellow, Olli," Dee continued like she hadn't heard Olli.

"Because-" Olli started.

"You're wearing pants. Olli, girls your age do not wear pants. Especially the girls of your status. Your father is the owner of this business, your family practically built this city from the ground up. You should be attending balls and dinner parties. But instead you're running around the shadiest parts of town in...pants." Dee paused to take and break and glanced over at Olli.

Olli was staring at Dee, her face contorted in something that looked like horror. "Dee, you know high society parties are *not* where I belong."

Dee folded her arms and frowned.

Olli shook her head pointedly. "Besides, I need to wear pants."

Dee shot her an exasperated look. "But dark grey and black pants? And why are they always wrinkled below your knees?" Dee pointed to the zig-zagging, deep wrinkles that were always present on Olli's pants legs from nearly her knees down to the cuffs.

Olli looked down at the bottom of her charcoal pants. A small smirk flitted across her face. She focused on Dee again. "Anything else you'd like to address while you're at it?" she asked, contained mirth sparkling behind her grey-green eyes.

"Yes. Yes I do." Dee walked forward and her right forefinger set down on the tip of Olli's right boot.

"My boots." Olli's eyebrows rose slightly.

"Boots. Girls your age don't wear boots unless it snows, and that's *only* while they're outside. Girls your age wear heels. Like these." Dee held her left hand out flat and a simple black heel with a little strap that would tie just under Olli's ankle appeared on her open palm. It had a heel that was about two inches tall, thick and sensible.

"My boots are black." Olli offered, trying to draw a parallel.

"And terribly scuffed." Dee shook her head.

"I use them." Olli grinned. She took her feet off the desk and stood up, her wrinkled from the knee down pants, falling down around her ankles. Olli stepped around her desk and leaned against the near edge. "And what do you suggest instead?" she wondered, her hands settling on the molding of the old mahogany desk on either side of her.

Dee looked thoughtful for a moment and pursed her lips. "Something like this." Dee looked to her right, the shoe zapping out of existence as she turned.

A full-size image of Olli appeared next to Dee. Only the holographic Olli wasn't wearing anything near what real Olli was. The hologram was in a rosey pink dress suit. The skirt fell to the middle of the hologram's shins, and her feet were clad in the same heels as the shoe that Dee had just been holding. Over the skirt was a neat little blaser that clung tightly to the hologram's ribs. The shoulders were tight and the sleeves fitted. "See? Aren't you pretty?" Dee started the hologram slowly turning and looked away to the real Olli.

Olli was staring at the image
askance. "I'm so pale! Dee, I look
dead!" She looked at her secretary, her
mouth open slightly. "Look at me, Dee. I
look like I've been dressed for my own
funeral." Olli shook her head, a smile
on her face despite her protests. "I
could never wear that. Where would I put
my badge?" she asked, standing up and
folding her arms as she stood up and
looked over the image of herself.

Dee frowned. "You look so
beautiful, Olli. Maybe not this color.
Perhaps a yellow?" The color of the
dress suit blinked to a sunny yellow and
continued to spin. "You could do your
job just as well in this," Dee
admonished, sending the image walking
around the office.

Olli watched the image of herself
walk past the coat stand, where her
black leather jacket hung; waiting for
the next adventure, and the tall mirror
by the door. Her holographic self then
walked down the length of the bare wall
opposite Olli's desk. Olli settled on
the arm of the closest of two black
leather arm chairs that faced her desk
and propped her chin on her right hand-
her elbow braced against the chair back-
as the image walked past the outside
wall of the office. The entire wall was
made up of four windows. Glass extended
from the ceiling to the floor, eight
feet tall by four feet wide. The glass
panes fitted seamlessly together, and
were extremely strong. Holographic Olli

then walked back to stand next to Dee, her right shoulder slipping past four filing cabinets that rested against the remaining wall of the office. The hologram stopped next to Dee and smiled at the real Olli.

Olli pursed her lips and looked at Dee. "I can't wear that." She stood up and walked closer to the hologram. "Is that wool?" Her lips pulled back in half-terror. "Oh, I'm itchy already." She shivered and shook her head.

Dee half-glared at Olli and frowned. "Fine. I'll wear it." The image of Olli disappeared and the dress suit and heels zapped onto Dee, replacing the simple blue day dress that she had been wearing. A second later the color changed from yellow to the original rosey pink.

Olli smiled. "That looks good on you. Let me tell you what it's like outside the building. Since you've never been."

"You mean, where girls wear things like this?" Dee asked, pulling down on the blaser a little bit.

Olli pursed her lips and barely shook her head. "Girls who don't do what I do for a living, yes."

"And what exactly is it that you can't do in a dress?" Dee asked, folding her arms.

Olli stood up and grinned. "Dee, do you know what a ladder looks like?"

Dee looked insulted. "Do I know what a ladder looks li-really Olli." the

15

image of a ladder appeared between the two girls.

Olli chuckled slightly. "Try to climb it now, and like someone is chasing you."

Dee looked at her like she was crazy. "Me?"

Olli shrugged. "You can run a simulation of someone dressed like you if you like."

Holograph Olli was back in an instant, wearing the same yellow outfit. She started up the ladder but was quickly bogged down by her inability to get her feet high enough for the rungs. Her jacket slid up and the material dug into her arms when she tried to reach for the next rung. Rips appeared at the seams on the shoulders of the blaser.

"If someone was chasing her, she'd be caught already. She hasn't even made it a third of the way up yet," Olli intoned from the other side of the struggling image.

Dee moved the image from between them and narrowed her eyes. "Fine, but that can't be all you do."

"I run a lot." Olli offered. "Have you ever run in a dress and heels, Dee?"

Dee looked at her like it was a stupid question. "What would I need to run for?" she asked, incredulous. "I can zap myself where I please."

Olli shrugged. "Do a simulation. Oh, and make sure that the ground isn't perfectly level too."

Holographic Olli started running

and almost instantly was tripping over the skirt that was wrapping around her legs. She stumbled and fell.

"Annnnnnnnnd she's caught again That didn't take long." Olli gestured to the still-prone holograph.

"So this is why you insist on wearing pants?" Dee glanced at the image and then focused back on Olli just before it disappeared.

Olli started back around her desk and flopped, very unceremoniously, and quite unladylike, into her chair. "Yes. But more importantly I can do this." Olli's right boot heel dropped heavily onto the top of her desk and then her left ankle dropped onto her right.

Dee stared at her for a moment. "*That* is hardly the most important thing you can do because of your pants."

Olli grinned and shrugged. She picked up the crime lord's file again. "Now. Where was I?"

"Paperwork, Olli, paperwork. Start with that daily report right there." Dee pointed to one of the stacks.

Olli sighed. "Fiiiiine," She drew out the word, throwing her head back and rolling her eyes at the ceiling. Her gaze shifted to Dee for a minute, and she picked up the daily report and stuffed the file back in it's drawer. She flopped back into her chair, pushing the drawer closed with her left foot it then dropped back into place over her right ankle.

"Thank you. I appreciate it." Dee

nodded, relieved that the conversation didn't end in Olli grabbing her black leather jacket and leaving the office until the next day.

Olli ignored Dee and re-adjusted her feet up on her scuffed-up, paper-weighted desk, settled deeper into her black leather chair and decidedly started reading a daily report. The detective number on the top was new, which piqued her interest. She was about to ask Dee to bring up the file when her office suddenly lit up with a red flashing light, and the wall across from Olli's desk parted down the middle and slid to either side, revealing the flat screened computer behind it. The screen was nearly as tall and as long as the wall. Olli sat up straighter, excitement sparkling in her eyes, and looked at the computer, which was blinking red.

Dee started to turn to the computer.

"I've got it." Olli pulled her feet off her desk and sat up. "Yes?"

The computer screen flashed red once more, and then Alan, the president and owner of WDA, Wainwright Detective Agency, blinked on.

"Sir?" Olli asked, standing up and walking around to the front of her desk and leaning against it. Something was happening. When her father talked to her after an alarm, it was something huge.

"Olli, it appears we have a detective in a little trouble," Alan informed.

Olli's eyebrows rose for a second and she nodded.

"Control Tower sent Detective 2748 to The District." Alan told her, tenting his fingers.

Olli glanced at her open door. There was a brass plate that was inscribed and glued to the door at about eye level. **Olivia Wainwright, District Detective.** Control should have notified her that there was something going on in The District. She tipped an eyebrow at it and turned to Alan.

Dee snorted and folded her holographic arms. She was of the firm opinion that the three computers that made up the Control Tower and kept tabs on the detectives out of WDA on cases were slow and worthless.

Olli glanced at Dee in warning, and looked back at her boss. "When?"

"About two hours ago." Alan looked at her, gauging her reaction. He knew that look. "Olli, I understand your displeasure at being notified this late, but now that you have been, you can move on," Alan intercepted.

Olli pursed her lips then nodded. "Yes, Sir. Where did Control lose track of 2748?"

"Just past Last Street." Alan's image blipped out for an aerial map of The District and the surrounding streets. A little flashing red dot indicated where 2748 had lost contact.

Olli blinked. She studied the map for a moment, until Alan's face appeared on the computer screen again. Olli tapped her chin with her right forefinger. She was surprised and a little miffed that the detective had gotten that far in the first place.

The corners of Alan's mouth turned up fondly for a second. "You should have been notified," Alan agreed. "And you have been now."

Olli slowly nodded. "You want me to go in and find him?"

Alan smiled and tilted his chair back. "I would be appreciative. And thank you for handling this the way you are." He smiled fondly again.

"You're welcome. I'm pretty sure I know where to start looking. I'll bring him back in one piece. Don't worry." Olli rolled her shoulders. She surprised herself at how well she was taking the news. The District was a dangerous place for anyone who didn't know what they were getting into.

"Good girl. I expect a full report when you return." Alan nodded in satisfaction, and the computer went black and the wall slid shut with finality.

Olli was already half-way across her office. The coat stand that was just to the right of the door rocked like a pendulum, nearly tipping past the point of balance as Olli snagged her leather jacket. She somehow managed to catch sight of the stand's precarious position just before she was completely out the door. Olli caught the stand scarcely before it hit the floor; she set it upright with a stay motion from her hands and darted out the doorway a moment later. While she ran down the hallway, past the elevator, heading for the stairs, she fought her arms into their leather casings. She snapped the jacket up onto her shoulders and jerked the bottom of the zipper together as she traversed the first few stairs without looking at them. A moment later the zipper whined as she roughly pulled it halfway up. "Dee, I'm going to need Monte for this one. Call him in, would you?" The small microphone hidden in her collar transmitted her message.

"Already did," came Dee's voice in her left ear.

Olli winced and nearly missed the next step. That was louder than normal. She pressed her finger into her ear and moved the receiver to a more comfortable position. Somehow, despite her nearly-lost balance, she managed to jump onto the banister that ran down the middle of the flight. Her progress was instantly sped up.

"You're in a good mood today," Dee mused.

Olli hit the floor of the second level. Her pace was forced to a brisk walk. "I'm sorry?" she questioned, starting to slip through the slower-moving detectives.

Dee smirked. She could see Olli's progress on the computer. "Normally you would have been in a short, determined mood, like the last time you had to fetch a detective out of The District,"

Dee shrugged.

Olli roughly brushed around a much bigger detective, knocking some papers out of his hands and splattering an annoyed look across his face. "Sorry," she called back over her shoulder. She jumped onto the banister two steps down the flight. "The last detective that I had to take out of The District was trying to prove that he could handle it. Something else is going on here. Breaking rules is something to get upset about. I'm not sure this is yet." Olli was finally down in the lobby . She burned through the room at a fast walk. She would have preferred to go faster, but at the speed she moving; it was easier to stop and navigate around the clumps of people walking. She couldn't help smirking to herself as the detectives and secretaries quickly started looking busier than they had been and nodded to her with happy smiles. She pushed through the right revolving door and out into the semi-grey light that hung over Big Town. The weather report had mentioned a chance for rain, and it was beginning to look like it was going to rain after all.

Olli glanced around once she was halfway between WDA and the curb. There was a hack sitting at the curb. It appeared to be waiting for her, but it wasn't the hack she was expecting. The cabbie wasn't wearing a hat. Monte *always* wore a cowboy hat. Olli was about to protest the inconvenient cabbie change but thought better of it. She didn't have the time to wait for Monte to get to her if he was busy enough to miss coming to pick her up. She would just have to convince this driver to take her to The District. Olli briskly walked up to the back door of the hack and opened it. She slid into the back seat and snapped the door shut behind her.

"Where to, Miss?" the balding cabbie wondered, looking at her in the rearview mirror. His tired blue eyes narrowed when he had to sit up straighter to see her. She was bent down toward the floor.

"Last Street," Olli replied, her voice muffled because she was looking at the floor. She glanced up from where she was frantically loosening the laces on her boots. The top was nearly to her knee, and the laces went all the way up. "Step on it," she added noticing the cabbie's sudden reluctance to take off. She pulled the black leather apart slightly and half pulled her left leg out of the boot. She wrapped her pant leg tightly around her calf and stuffed it back into her boot.

"That be a rough part of town, there, Missy," the cabbie protested, merging into traffic. "Why-"

"Last Street, please. On the double, Man, it's important!" Olli interrupted, firmly. It wasn't that she didn't appreciate the fact that the cabbie was worried about her safety enough to try to talk her into moving her destination to someplace "safer". It was simply that she didn't have enough time to try rationalizing with him. She pulled on the laces and began to tighten them from her ankle up.

"You must have a death wish, Missy." The cabbie reluctantly turned down the next street that would lead to Last Street.

Olli nodded, but didn't look up from tightening her laces. She quickly tied a tight bow at the top and stuck the extra in her boot.

Chapter 2

Olli leaned back against the backrest, once she had finished doing the same thing to her right pant leg, and watched impatiently as the neighborhood started to go from businesses that were thriving to those shadier and less-frequented. She was one of three people in Big Town who weren't terrified of Last Street and what it represented. Alan Wainwright and his estranged partner, Jake Bently, were District Detectives when Olli was little. Although Jake had disappeared years earlier, Olli still believed that her 'Uncle' was alive somewhere. Therefore, she counted him as one of the three. The District Detectives, both past and present, knew that Last Street was probably safer for everyone than Main Street for the simple reason that, more often than not, Last Street was completely deserted.

Last Street came into view, and the hack suddenly pulled to the side of the road and stopped. "This is the end of the road, Missy; I isn't gettin' any closer to that God-forsaken place," the driver informed firmly. It seemed that he had paled a few shades since Olli had looked at him a moment or two before.

Olli glanced through the windshield. Last Street was still a good two hundred yards off at least. But she smiled reassuringly, took some bills out of her inside pocket, peeled four off and handed them to the cabbie. It was two and half dollars more than the fare, but she felt he deserved it. He had gotten closer than she was expecting him to. "For your trouble. Keep the change." She stuffed the remaining bills into her inside pocket, opened the door, stepped out and closed it in one smooth motion. She walked away from the hack, flipping her collar to the wind and zipping her jacket a little higher. It smelled like it was going to rain soon.

The hack suddenly took off, tires squealing, the rear end sliding around, pointing the nose back toward the way that they had come. Once straightened out, the hack pulled away, heading back to civilized Big Town--and more reasonable people.

Olli turned around and walked backwards a couple steps to watch the hack disappear around the corner. She turned back around with a half-skip and started toward the buildings with a long, quick stride. She took a deep breath and sighed in contentment. This

was where she belonged. Th
e District. Ever since she was a little
girl, Olli had been fascinated with The
District. She would beg for stories from
her father, Jake or her grandfather
every chance she would get--much to her
late mother's chagrin. Olli was snapped
out of her thoughts of times long ago as
she got close to The Line. Not that The
Line was actually a physical line. It
ran down the middle of Last Street; the
place where Big Town city limits ended
and The District began. Something
suddenly felt off. The closer she got,
the more Olli could feel the tenseness
grow. It soon got to the point she could
almost taste it. The entire District
seemed to hold its breath in
anticipation of something. Olli stopped.
It felt like The District was watching
for something. She quickly moved over to
the shadows of an old tenement building
and eased into the darkness of a
doorway. She didn't like the sound of
the silence that shrouded The District.
Olli reached back her memory; as far
back as she could remember, The District
had never had such explosive silence. It
made her jittery and tense. Olli edged
carefully down the wall of the tenant
building and glanced down Last Street to
her left and then peered around the
corner of the building to her right.
There weren't any cars coming, not that
there should have been. But Olli was not
only looking around to make sure that
she was absolutely alone, but she was

trying to decide which way to start looking for 2748. Control had lost contact almost three hours before, and The District was a big place. She highly doubted that 2748 was still on Last Street. Olli glanced directly across Last Street at a shady alley. She had seen it many times, but today her imagination, which was running in overdrive, made her feel like there was someone hiding in the shadows watching her every move, ready to push the detonating button on the silence if she made a wrong move. She zipped around the corner and ducked into a shadowed overhang to keep out of sight and a perfectly still watch. "Dee, where exactly did Control lose contact with 2748?" Olli wondered, her voice so low it was barely audible.

"Stand by. Control is trying to keep from releasing the information," Dee's voice answered in Olli's left ear. "You know, I could do twice as good as those three computers combined," Dee muttered in annoyance as she and Olli waited.

Olli smirked in amusement. Dee never missed the chance to take a jab at Control's computers. "I could use why 2748 was sent here in the first place. There has to be a reason." Her eyes darted to and probed the shadows making sure that they were empty.

It was quiet for a while.

"Olli, Control sent him down to answer a break-in call at 25 EW South. Start there and follow those hunches you always seem to have," Dee came back finally after almost two minutes.

Olli snorted despite herself. Dee was always skeptical of her hunches. "Thank you, Dee." She hurried down Last Street, ducking in and out of shadows. She was almost to the call spot when something dawned on her. She stopped in a small hallway-like alley between two tenant houses and flattened against the wall in shadow. "25 EW South. That was a hardware store... Handy Randy's. It's been closed for twenty-some years, right?"

"It will never cease to amaze me how you know where places are in there. Yes, it was indeed Handy Randy's. It's been closed for twenty-five years and four months to be exact," Dee agreed.

"A break-in alarm. Hmm. What _is_ going on upstairs?!" Olli narrowed her eyes. She darted out of the alley she was in and slid easily into the shadows in an alley a building down on the other side of the street. Olli cut around the next building and came to a halt behind a broken-down flatbed truck that was across from Handy Randy's.

Nothing was moving. The building looked like it had indeed been abandoned for a quarter of a century. The paint was chipping off the sign and the rest of the building. Olli turned so she was facing The District. A suspicion was starting to form in her mind. Two-Timer's headquarters wasn't too far from the point where she now stood. It was no secret how much Two-Timer hated the detectives from WDA whether they were District Detective or not, but a deeper burning hatred was reserved for new detectives. Olli didn't know how new 2748 was to the detective business, but she did know that WDA had many new detectives, and Alan had been employing new detectives fresh out of the academy lately. She jogged on down the street. After a couple of alleys, she stopped just short of a rusting fire escape and looked around to make sure that she was still alone. Once she was satisfied that she was, she started up. About halfway to the top, Olli slid through a broken window, carefully avoiding broken glass and other obstructions that had been left in the room. She ran through the room and flattened herself against the wall where the door would have been if it was still on its hinges. She glanced down the hall, first one way and then the other to make sure that there weren't any thugs wandering around that she would have to avoid. She then trotted down the hall to her right and slid down a banister to the lower level. Olli power-walked to where the hallway "T"ed into another hallway. Once she was sure the coast was still clear, she flipped a nearby switch.

The solid wall across the hall shivered for a second and then slowly swung inward without a sound. Beyond the wall was a hallway that disappeared into darkness as it sloped back down toward the street.

Olli walked quickly in and flipped the switch on the inside wall. She stepped out of the way of the silent wall as it swung back into position and blinked once because of the dim light that suddenly clicked on when the wall was completely closed. Now Olli was completely sealed off from Dee. But that didn't worry her. She had run around in The District long before she was District Detective; she knew where she was going, and she didn't need Dee to inform her while she was in the tunnels. Olli started off down the hallway at a brisk trot.

The hallway gradually started to flatten out and soon it was completely level. This meant that the street was just above Olli's head. The tunnel took a few winding turns here and there and then started to slant up. Soon the slant turned into stairs, and Olli wondered what it would be like if she could slide up the banister as she jogged up the many steps. Soon she reached the landing and the short hallway that was beyond it. She walked the last couple of feet to yet another light switch. She flipped it on. As the wall slid back into itself, the lights blinked off. Olli poked her head out of the opening and looked around. The hallway was on the fourth floor of Two-Timer's headquarters. She stepped out and closed the wall behind her, confusion narrowing her eyes. She had used that door more times than she could remember and every time she had to be extremely careful not to walk right into a thug or hitman walking past. Today there wasn't anyone pacing the hallway. She wasn't sure if that was a good sign or a bad one, but she took it as it was and started toward the stairs at the end of the hall. There was nothing here that suggested prisoners. The flight of stairs was short, and Olli decided it would be just as fast to walk down as it would have been to slide down the short banister. She started down. She stopped for a second, mid-way between two steps, cocking her head. She thought she heard something, but since nothing else was making noise, she shrugged it off and started down again.

Suddenly leather squeaked on the leather of her jacket, and a tight grip settled on Olli's arm just above her left elbow.

Olli stopped and slowly looked down at the black leather glove on her arm. She <u>had</u> heard something. Olli smiled tightly. It was bound to happen sooner or later. She hadn't been caught in a while, but she really didn't have time for this today. "All right. You got me this time, what do you say we chalk this up to you and you let me go without making me escape…just for the fun of it. What do you say, Two…" Olli's voice drifted off in her surprise as she turned around. She was looking at a tall, burly man in an expensive suit and fedora. His dark completion was almost glowing with pleasure. He had a leather strap over his right shoulder attached to a Tommy gun. It wasn't Two-Timer at all.

"You really stirred it up this time, Doll," he informed her, smiling in satisfaction. He even sounded pleased.

"Ace?" Olli spluttered, trying not to look too confused. The last thing she needed to do was give him the satisfaction of seeing her all tied in knots.

"The one and only," Ace agreed. His smirk was too happy for his normally sullen, easily set-off temper.

"Have you and Two-Timer finally broken your hate pact?" Olli wondered, casually looking down at his hand out of the corner of her eye. Maybe she could distract him enough to get out of his grip, then dodge the ensuing detective search, and still find 2748 while she was at it.

"I'm just here to talk. It's a pity to turn a Doll like you over to that fink. But I suppose it is his place." Ace tightened his grip on Olli's arm just after she tried to jerk it out of his hand.

"You're just saying that," Olli pshawed, tilting her head away, pretending to be embarrassed. In all reality, she was attempting to figure out how to get away now that her arm-escape seemed a little more difficult than she was planning on. The grip he had was a little tighter than she would have preferred, but if she was going to get away, she was just going to have to work around that.

"Let's go for a little walk, shall we, Doll?" Ace suggested, motioning her down the stairs with his left hand, and then nudging her with his right elbow when Olli hesitated.

"I'd rather not, if it's all the same to you," Olli protested slightly, stalling.

"Let's go, Doll," Ace growled a little. "Got to show you to that fink." He pushed her a little hard, and then stiffened his arm so she wouldn't fall head-long down the last four steps.

Olli walked down the last couple of stairs and allowed Ace to steer her toward a door behind which Two-Timer's office waited. "Why? It seems to me that you've never been one to follow the rules of conduct," she muttered the jab, not wanting the guard in the pin-stripe suit to hear it.

Ace opened the door and motioned her through with a jerk of his head. "It is a tempting thought to give the rat a taste of his own medicine, but not today."

"Good for you, being the bigger man," Olli praised. She knew it was probably a bad idea, but she couldn't keep the comment to herself.

Ace glanced darkly at her for a moment but let it slide. He had more important things to deal with at the moment.

Two-Timer's office was big. The walls were white, pinned with maps of different places in The District. An expensive area rug that covered the floor just under the two brown leather chairs that faced the huge mahogany desk and the brown leather desk chair that sat behind the desk. It was in this chair that the fink himself, Two-Timer, sat. He stood up, leaning his hands on his polished desk. His entire chiseled face smiled at Olli like a kid who had the run of the candy store.

Olli smiled slightly at him. She plunked down on the floor when Ace pushed her down. "Bracelets? Really? I won't go anywhere, Ace, I promise," Olli protested in a hurt voice as she watched Ace snap the handcuff on her right wrist and cinch it down. Of course it wasn't true. If Ace had indeed left Olli unattended, she would have disappeared almost instantly. Despite the fact that Olli knew that Ace wasn't fooled by her little charade, she thought it was worth a shot.

"You're lucky you're worth more to us alive, Doll," Ace snarled looking back over his shoulder at her as he walked toward Two-Timer's desk.

Olli moved a little to her right, trying to find a more comfortable position, and bumped her shoulder against something. She slowly looked over and found her shoulder against a bicep incased in brown leather. She followed it up to a broad shoulder. From there she looked at his face. He couldn't have been more than three years older than she was. Dried blood smeared across his square-cut jaw and up to a nasty cut just above his left eyebrow. He was out cold. Olli cocked her head and tipped an eyebrow. *Wonder what he's here for?* She mused to herself, shifting so she could see his face a little better. *He doesn't seem the type to work for Ace or Two-Timer.* His face had an honest look about it. *They sure slammed him into something. He's going to have a nasty headache.*

"Brute, keep an eye on our visitor. She tends to get feisty," Two-Timer informed the room behind Olli, still grinning at her.

Olli noticed that Two-Timer was looking past her, and she slowly turned to see who he was talking to. Her eyes the last to turn. She wasn't too pleased with what she saw. He was huge, thick-set and the Tommy gun appeared to grow out of his meaty hands. His slit eyes peered at Olli and sent an involuntary shiver up her spine. Olli didn't have to stretch her mind very far to come up with the way he earned his name. There was no way she was going to be able to take on the behemoth with or without the help of her unconscious fellow prisoner. Olli shot a fake grin, with all of her teeth showing, toward him; her lips pulled away from her teeth. She lost interest in the guard. It wasn't going to get her anywhere, anyway, and it interested and worried her that Ace was at Two-Timer's in the first place. She shifted again so she could easily see the desk. Ace and Two Timer were both sitting on the edge of their chairs, nodding and easily carrying on a conversation. Two-Timer caught Olli looking at him and grinned his best slippery-fish grin. Olli frowned a little; she knew it was because he was sure that she wasn't going to be able to cause any trouble while he and Ace negotiated who got to hold her. Until Alan was forced to come looking for her. Unfortunately for them, Olli wasn't too keen on watching them argue over her. "Two-Timer, could I possibly have something to clean him up?" She tilted her head toward the prisoner on the floor next to her.

Chapter 3

The two crime lords turned to look at her like she was interrupting an armistice. For almost a full minute, it seemed like they were going to deny Olli's request and enjoy the feeling of telling her so.

Olli shrugged and nodded to her fellow prisoner. "In my defense, you boys still haven't learned to clean up your messes." Her head tipped pointedly toward the blood.

Two-Timer stared at her testily for a moment and then nodded to Brute, who exited the room for a minute. "We let you Wainwrights clean up your own. Don't want to get our hands dirty."

Olli blinked. She wasn't ready for that answer. She watched as Brute lowered a shallow bowl of water between them. She looked back at Two-Timer. "Thank you."

"Anything for you," Two-Timer smiled. It was the kind of oily smile that would make any person wonder exactly what the man was thinking about when he said it.

Olli paused with the cloth in mid-air and raised her eyebrows. 'That was unnecessary.' She shook her head and wrung the cloth out good so it wouldn't drip. She was rubbing off the blood on his jaw when the entire meaning of what Two Timer had said dawned on her. Olli pulled back for a second. So this was 2748? That didn't seem right. Olli didn't know what she was expecting, but she was not expecting him to look like that. Olli wasn't sure why, but she never really expected him to be handsome. She shrugged slightly, then dipped the cloth back into the water and wrung it out. She started working on the blood that had trickled past his eye. *I wonder what color they are,* Olli idly wondered as she glanced at his still-closed eyelids. *There are more important things to worry about right now, Olli*, her more sensible half reminded.

Everything on the desk jumped and clattered as Two-Timer's fist slammed into the hard wood. "…My headquarters, therefore she's mine!" he stated vehemently.

"But you were so busy gloating over Little Boy Blue here that I caught her. She's mine," Ace asserted, standing up and leaning his hands on the edges of the desk. He didn't look the least bit impressed with his opponent's tantrum.

Olli looked past 2748 at them for a second. She didn't like the way their conversation was starting to go. This was more like what Ace and Two-Timer normally acted like when they actually took the time to 'talk'. She really didn't want to see the way this little war ironed itself out, but no grand escape plans were coming to mind. Olli looked back at 2748 in time to see his head shift a little. She folded the cloth up into a long strip and laid it on his forehead and watched his face. Her grey-green eyes locked into his hazels when they opened. She blinked quickly; she didn't want him to think that she was staring right at him. That would be awkward.

He blinked a couple of times and then squinted at her. "Where-?" He looked up at the light fixture and then he looked at her again, this time with only his left eye open. "Where am I?" He asked in a thick southern accent.

Olli smiled slightly. The accent fit him somehow. "In a crime lord's office, in a pair of bracelets, with a guard, and two short-tempered crime lords arguing imprisonment rights." Olli frowned past him toward Ace and Two-Timer, who were glaring murderously at each other. "How's your head?" Olli flipped the cloth over. She was barely talking above a whisper, but she still felt like she was bellowing at him. After a quick glance in the direction of the crime bosses across the room, she was relieved to see that they hadn't noticed that 'Little Boy Blue' was awake yet. That can of worms could be opened up later. They had enough to argue about at the moment.

He watched his left arm pick up as she switched the cloth. "It smarts a bit." He picked up his arm a little when he noticed the handcuff dug into her right wrist as she placed the cloth on his forehead.

Olli felt the weight lift off her right wrist, and along with it came the overwhelming tide of self-consciousness. She slowly took the cloth away and smiled slightly at him when he glanced at her. She dropped the cloth into the bowl. If she didn't look at him for a minute or two, she wouldn't have to see the puzzled look on his face, and hopefully he would miss the slight blush that was creeping up her cheeks. Switching back into her observation mode, Olli glanced at Ace and Two-Timer. They were staring each other down intensely. That was bound to end badly. She glanced at the wall across from them, wishing there was a way to get through it. She narrowed her eyes for a second. *There's a fire escape right there. If only I could get to it!*

"Tryin' to burn a hole through that wall, Ma'am?" the southern accent wondered.

Olli shrugged. "There's a fire escape on the other side of that wall somewhere, and it's just begging to be escaped on." She watched his reaction out of the corner of her eye. She hadn't missed the slight teasing note in the accent.

A crooked smile popped up on his face, and his hazel eyes sparkled. "There's a coupla singe marks right there, see 'em?" he teased quietly, the corners of his mouth twitched slightly.

Olli looked at the wall for a second, and leaned over so her shoulder was pressing into his arm again. "Actually, I think that's a fly." She sat up again, watching out of the corner of her eye again.

His eyebrows rose for a second and the crooked smile flashed. *Very well done. Interesting.*

Ace and Two-Timer suddenly stood straighter and started snapping out sentences. They were losing control on their tempers pretty fast. Brute started to get distracted by the two crime gurus arguing heatedly. Ace was making sharp hand gestures, trying to make a point, and Two-Timer was interrupting with hand gestures and counter-points.

Olli glanced at them apprehensively and then looked distractedly back at the wall. "I don't suppose you have any great escape plans?" she wondered, hoping they might get lucky.

His head slowly shook. "Oh no. Any escape plan I could possibly come up with pales in the light of your brilliant burn-through-the-wall plan."

Olli didn't have anything to say to that. It was a compliment of sorts, and yet not completely. She looked at him and sighed. She looked past him toward the desk, willing them to threaten each other longer.

"Now don't go burnin' a hole in it yet, I might be onto somethin'," he

protested, his eyes sparkling as he
started to try to get something out of
his back pocket with his right hand.
There was nothing he could do. He just
couldn't stop himself from teasing her a
little more.

Olli opened her mouth to defend
herself but decided against it and
turned back to the wall. She couldn't
help a small smile; he was a smart
aleck, but he definitely made the
situation a whole lot more interesting.
Her attention was torn away from the
wall when suddenly it seemed as if The
Great War resumed over their captivity
at Two-Timer's desk.

The detectives looked at the desk
together and then at each other
apprehensively. Olli leaned closer to
him and turned her face a little so that
Brute couldn't see her lips move.
"What's your name?" she asked, barely
breaking above a whisper.

"Dallas," he answered, glancing at
the two yelling at each other by the
desk. "You?"

"It's-" Olli started.

"...Olivia Wainwright!" Ace and Two-
Timer had their faces thrust at each
other now, veins straining against the
skins of their foreheads. Neither one
was interested in the protests of the
other, nor were they going to let it go.
Brute was starting to get more worried
about his boss than he was about the two
prisoners in his charge. They were
sitting quietly enough.

"Like the man said." Olli shrugged.

He suddenly slipped his hand into hers and pulled it toward him.

"What?" Olli hissed. It was the only coherent thing that she could hiss at the moment. Many other sentences had come to mind, but there were so many bouncing around in her head that she couldn't figure out what to say.

"Just a minute. <u>Please</u> be quiet." Dallas glanced at her like she was over-reacting. He understood her indignant look and her hot whisper, but there were more important things to worry about at the moment.

Olli nodded slightly. "Sure." Then she saw the straightened paper clip that he was hiding in his right hand. *Picking the locks. Aces!* It was a good idea. The longer she sat next to him, the more she doubted that he was anything but a seasoned detective. She glanced at the desk in time to see Ace pull a derringer out of somewhere she couldn't see.

Ace looked pointedly at the derringer when Two-Timer didn't see at it right away. This did not improve the overall feeling of love between the two of them. Two-Timer, not to be outdone, slid a pearl-handled derringer out of his sleeve. Things were starting to get downright nasty. The two crime lords stared at each other, daring the other to pull the trigger. That's when Two-Timer off-handedly pointed the barrel in Olli's direction, like he really wasn't trying to aim at her head, but since it was in the way, no hard feelings.

Olli glanced around, trying to figure out an escape from this new development. Much to her chagrin, she was stuck. There wasn't anywhere to go; Two-Timer had too straight a shot. They had her shoved practically into the corner of the room. She couldn't duck down fast enough; she would pull Dallas with her and he might get shot instead. Two-Timer was grasping at straws if he thought that he could threaten Ace with her death. She couldn't help a slight sigh of relief when Two-Timer pointed his gun at Ace again. Two-Timer and Ace weren't going to kill each other. Despite how much they wanted the other dead, it would never be in a scenario like the one at the desk. It was too messy. They would want it to look like an accident. Olli knew that it was extremely unlikely that they would kill each other at this particular moment, but she watched, fascinated, just in case they did. When their yelling stopped, suddenly she glanced down to see how Dallas was doing on the locks. The paperclip stopped mid-twist and slipped up into Dallas' leather jacket. The next instant his hand slid out of hers. Olli looked up and saw Ace barreling toward them. A quick glance toward the desk showed Two-Timer, slowly sitting up, wiping blood away from a large cut just above his eye.

"Get up. We're leaving now!" Ace snapped. He barely waited for them to start to scramble to their feet. His meaty hand reached down and snatched the middle of the cuffs and hauled them up. The next moment he was shoving them toward the door, which he jerked open quickly.

The two shots that chased the three of them out of the office were stopped by the door which Ace slung shut behind them. A blistering trail of splintering wood cut down the door from Brute's Tommy gun. By now Olli and Dallas were almost halfway down the stairs they had been haphazardly shoved toward. But that wasn't good enough for Ace. His attempts to push them faster did nothing but upset their already barely-held-together balance. Suddenly they reached the bottom of the stairs and stumbled onto the level floor of the empty warehouse. There was nothing in the room that could even pose as cover between the stairs and the door that lead to the outside world far to their left.

For a split second Olli actually worried that Ace was going to push them across the empty room, but she should have given him more credit.

Ace pushed them toward the wall straight ahead of them. A few feet from the wall, the floor opened up and Olli caught a glimpse of another flight of stairs over Dallas' shoulder before he was pushed down the stairs and she was forced to follow. She trotted down the stairs and ducked a floor joist. The floor under the stairs disappeared out of the shaft of light that shot down like a wide bolt of lightning. The fact that it was dark in the tunnel, or hall, didn't dampen her enthusiasm for the new-found escape route.

Olli stepped carefully behind Dallas, not exactly sure where she was in relation to him, but she knew that she wasn't too distant because her right arm wasn't stretched out too far in front of her. She turned almost completely around and walked sideways when gunfire erupted behind them. Ace stood about three steps from the bottom, flashes of light sparking off the metal handrails next to him. The muzzle of his Tommy gun spat fire as he started firing back. Olli turned back around just in time to walk right into a muscular back encased in leather. She closed her eyes for a second and sighed slightly. "Aces!" She muttered.

"Sorry, Ma'am, after you." Dallas somehow managed to slip his hand into hers on the first try. As he pulled her past him, he stepped in behind her, shielding her with his body.

Olli looked back over his shoulder just in time see Ace flip a switch next to the handrail and the shaft of light began to disappear quickly as the wall shut.

"Get moving!" Ace howled at them, as he caught up to them.

Olli started off, walking blindly, biting her lip to keep from yelling back at Ace that if they 'hurried up' any more, she would pull both of them to the floor. She quickened her blind pace when a sudden whirring whipped past her shoulder. That was a bullet if there ever was one. Her left hand was stretched out carefully in front of her. Suddenly her hand ran into a hard wall so fast that her arm bent back. There was a slight light was coming from her right and she could see just how close Dallas had been to running into her. Dust puffed off the wall next to her, leaving dents in the brick. She cringed away.

"To your right! Move it, Doll!" Ace snarled, glancing back over his shoulder. Obviously he didn't think that anyone else knew about his tunnel. He turned back and fired back into the darkness. More bursts of light answered back instantly.

Olli turned to her right and squinted against the light that was shining brighter now than before. It looked like it was a door that had opened up in the outside wall. It was an opening in the wall, but it wasn't a door. It was at about Olli's shoulder, reminding her slightly of a fox hole. She seriously wondered if Ace would be able to get out through the narrow tunnel.

"Get up there!" Ace growled, jerking his head toward the shaft of light.

Olli looked at it and then at her right wrist. There was no way that they were going to be able to climb up the shaft with the handcuffs. "You're going to have to let us go!" Olli directed to Ace, ducking instinctively when gunfire spattered their direction.

"Go!" Ace didn't budge an inch. He fired past Olli's left shoulder into the darkness.

Chapter 4

Olli slammed up against Dallas' arm and shoulder, lifting her arm to protect her face. "There's no way we're going to get up there with these!" She jerked her right arm and pulled Dallas' up a little.

Ace fired another burst and pulled out the keys. "Don't even think about escaping," he barked, tossing the keys at Dallas.

Dallas snatched them out of the air and quickly unlocked her cuff, shielding her from the gunfire with his body as much as possible. As soon as her cuff opened, he cupped his hands and looked at her expectantly.

Olli quickly stuck her right foot into his hands and bounced a little. On the second bounce he pushed her up to the level of the shaft and inside a little. Her hands caught, as did her left knee, and she quickly scrambled up toward the outside world.

A moment after he was sure that she was going up, Dallas pulled himself up into the shaft, grunting when he nearly wedged his shoulders between the rough stone walls.

Olli was almost to the top when a black pin-stripe-suited sleeve with a hand reaching out of it came down almost to where she was. She couldn't see behind her, but she could still hear the gunfire, and, since escape was a subject for later, she grasped the hand and felt herself yanked from the hole.

"Stay!" Black Suit ordered with force.

Olli stumbled back and bumped into the running sedan that was sitting in the alley she was now standing in. For a moment she thought of jumping Black Suit while he was pulling Dallas up and then maybe the two of them could out-run Ace and his henchman. But the idea was a bad idea at best.

Ace was pulled out a moment later, and while Black Suit quickly hurried to the driver's seat on the other side of the sedan, he jerked the door open.

Olli hesitated for a moment, not sure if her running plan was really such a bad idea. But she hesitated too long.

Ace looked at her and pointed his Tommy gun at her. "Get in," he snarled.

Olli watched him until she slid into the back seat. She wasn't going to let him think that she was afraid of him. Olli slid far enough to let Dallas in. Despite their hasty efforts, when Ace forced the door shut, it still almost caught Dallas.

"Drive!" Ace ordered as soon as he opened his door. He jumped into his seat and closed the door as Black Suit put the car in gear and drove off, squealing the tires.

A black sedan came screaming around the corner, it's body rocked over on the left side tires.

Olli whipped around and looked over her shoulder at the other black sedan. She knew the two men in the front seat were Two-Timer's thugs. Her closed her eyes for a second in annoyance. "They couldn't just flip a coin. Oh no," she rolled her eyes, her voice low. The last thing she needed was for Ace to hear what she said.

Ace slowly turned around to look at her, his face covered with its usual angry mask. He hadn't heard specific words, but he had heard her voice. His derringer seemed to appear out of thin air in his hand, and he held it so there wasn't a doubt in Olli's mind that he was threatening her with it. Once he was sure that Olli understood just how dire a situation she was in, he turned back to his mirror to study the black sedan trailing them.

Olli's upper lip curled back as Ace looked away. She glared at him for a moment. There really wasn't anyone in The District or Big Town whom she despised more than Ace. The grudge she held against him was long and hardened.

Dallas was in the middle of twisting the key to open up the cuff that was still gripping his left wrist. He glanced at her face and his eyebrows rose. She didn't seem like the type who would do something out of hate, but it looked like she might jump the burly man in the front seat.

A burst of gunfire out through the air toward them. Olli and Dallas ducked slightly and looked back over their shoulders. They watched the passenger lean out the window and fire another burst of rounds at the sedan they were in. Olli turned to Dallas. She Looked at him.

Dallas knew instantly that she was hoping he had some great escape plan. Which he didn't. His lips pursed together and he barely shook his head. He ducked and threw a protecting arm across her shoulders when an especially big burst of gunfire came from the car behind them. Glass from the rear window sprayed over them.

Olli looked up in time to see Ace lean out the window and fire off a few bursts back at the trailing sedan. He cursed loud enough they could hear him when the spray missed the car behind them.

Gunfire peppered back, this time more insistent, making sure that everyone in the car knew that there was no giving up.

"They're getting closer," Olli gritted between her teeth at the same time Dallas muttered, "They're gaining on us."

Olli was now almost completely sure that Dallas wasn't a new detective. He wasn't the least bit jumpy; he had obviously been shot at before. If it were possible, it seemed that he was more concerned about her safety than anything.

His hazel eyes suddenly lit up and he Looked at her, his crooked smirk appearing again. Olli caught the look and her eyebrows rose. She was ready to get out of the car chase.

Dallas nodded to the driver pointedly, and then focused on the crime boss, who was leaning out the window again, firing back at the tailing car.

Olli slid into a better position behind Black Suit, and quickly decided what the best course of action was. She slowly slid forward until she was gripping tightly onto the edge of the seat. Olli glanced at Dallas for a second, checking to make sure that he was ready, and then began punishing Black Suit's ears and the side of his head with her fists and open palms. He angered instantly and began to hit back at her. Olli leaned back as far as she could and continued her onslaught. When he managed to get his hand in her hair, she went with his pull and socked his jaw as hard as she could, mentally cursing the feeling in her knuckles a minute later. Black Suit's attention steadily was pulled away from his driving. Soon the black sedan was narrowly missing the solid walls that lined the alley. Each swerved he sedan seemed to be getting a little closer to the wall, and the turns to avoid it were becoming sharper.

Ace's attention was drawn away from the tailing car after the second sharp, neck cracking swerve. He started to pull in; he didn't make it farther than opening his mouth to demand what was going on before a solid right cut him off. Ace swung the butt of his Tommy gun back around in an attempt to clip the detective who had dared to throw the punch.

Dallas ducked the arc of the gun butt, and then sent a hard left hook which contacted solidly with Ace's nose. Unfortunately he wasn't ready for the stiff right that cut across his chin and bottom lip.

Olli was having better luck with her end of the fight. She stood up as much as the car's ceiling would let her, and began to rain down blows from above, making sure to keep her head as far out of his grip as she possibly could. Olli froze when she heard the sound of a hammer pulling back. She slowly turned to her right, and found herself staring down a barrel of a handgun. She looked past it at Ace's now-bloody face. There was no doubt in her mind that the sights were right between her eyes, and that Ace would pull the trigger if she breathed wrong.

"Sit down," Ace ordered.

Olli obliged, stiffly, and slid slowly to the backrest of the back seat. There was absolutely nothing to be done about her current problem. Her eyes slowly shifted away from the barrel of the gun to Dallas, and then her eyes darted back to the barrel of the gun.

"That's more like it. Stay that way," Ace ordered with a growl.

Dallas wiped the blood away from his mouth with the back of his hand. He looked at Olli, a crooked smile ready to assure her that all was not lost when the hate and anger in her eyes stopped him.

"I know what you're thinking, Ace," Olli braved, her jaw muscles clenching. She was barely holding back her scream of frustration, and old painful memories were swooping into her head that she was trying, in vain, to block out.

Ace looked at her and smiled slightly. He looked at his handgun and smiled wickedly. "Why spoil a good run?" He started to squeeze his finger back around the trigger. "I've waited years for this day," His voice sounded almost gleeful.

"I think that's a good place to stop," Dallas announced, slamming into her suddenly, a split second before the shot. He was recoiling the next moment, and grabbed the gun in his left hand; he jerked Ace toward him and sent a terrifyingly hard right into his jaw, knocking him out. He heard another cock and looked at the driver who now had a derringer pointed at his head.

Olli had recovered from Dallas' tackle in time to see Ace's gun fall from his hand onto the floor just behind the seat. She picked it up, slipped on the safety and gripped the barrel. She sat up. "I'm pretty sure that you don't want to do that."

"No, I really think I do," Black Suit disagreed. He glanced quickly between the alley and Dallas without slowing down.

Olli pistol-whipped the driver with a little more force than necessary. She nodded in satisfaction when his eyes rolled back up into his head and he went slack. She looked down at the gun in her hand, and her upper lip curled back. She tossed it out the shattered back window and then glanced out the windshield. The sedan was now driverless, going faster, and heading straight for a mammoth brick wall.

"Down!" Dallas again tackled her, wrapping his left arm around her shoulders, and his right around her waist, covering her with his body. They were both thrown to the floor when the sedan hit the wall in an explosion of glass and metal. It screeched along the wall, bounced around a corner, finally scraping to a slow stop, its front end a mangled mess. A couple of seconds after the motion stopped, Dallas was up and pulling on Olli's hand. "Are you all right?"

Olli grunted and tried to work her way off the floor and pulled on Dallas' arm for support. "I think so."

Dallas nearly jerked her out of the back seat, but he caught her so she wouldn't fall. Once he was sure that she had her feet under her, he let her go.

Olli looked back the way they had come for a second, and then she started off toward a nearby door at a fast jog, Dallas right behind her. Olli jerked the door open as wide as she could throw it and bolted into the dark, cool interior of the warehouse. The entire floor was empty, but at the far back left corner, a set of metal stairs led up to the second level. The door banged shut when the detectives were well on their way to the stairs.

They pounded up the stairs, ran helter-skelter down a short hall, and turned to their left when the hall did, barely skidding to stop in time to keep from running down a barricade made of jumbled up desks and chairs. Bullet holes peppered the walls, crisscrossed the barricade, and drilled across the fire hose that hung coiled up on the left wall.

"Aces!" Olli snapped, looking for a way around the mass of wood. There was no way they were going to be able to scramble over it in time.

Their situation became a little more urgent when the sound of a car pulling up wafted through a broken window nearby.

"If only there was a way to send them off chasin' shadows." Dallas looked around trying to find some way to do that.

Olli started a little, and then

briskly walked into a room that was to her left. She reappeared a moment later, caught Dallas around the wrist and pulled him into the room she had just come from. "See that fire escape over there?" she asked, pointing through the broken window toward another room beyond the barricade.

Dallas looked where she pointed. The fire escape was badly rusted and looked like it might fall apart at any moment. He nodded, not sure where she was going with her plan.

"Fire escapes are my trademark getaways. <u>Every</u> thug in The District knows that. If we can make them <u>think</u> that we got to that fire escape, we can send them off on a wild goose chase," Olli explained.

Dallas' crooked smile popped up, and his hazel eyes sparkled. "The fire hose." He spun around and disappeared around the outside of the doorframe.

Olli looked out the window and caught a glimpse of the tail end of a sedan rounding the corner looking for them. They didn't have much more time. "Hurry, Dallas!" she hissed turning around in time to see him drop the hose out the window. She began to push on his chest. "We have to find somewhere to hide, fast. They're going to be in here any minute!"

Both detectives froze for a split second when the metallic sound of the door at the bottom of the warehouse floor banged open and hit the side of the building. Gunfire reverberated off the walls, jarring the detectives into action.

As footsteps started pounding across the floor, the detectives barreled out of the room, making as little noise as they possibly could. Once they were out of the room, they split up. There were two thugs, yelling back and forth at each other, confident that they had cornered their prey and they didn't have to sneak up on it.

Olli didn't see where Dallas went. She actually thought for a moment about cutting into the room on the right side of the hallway, but then she saw a crevice between a desk and a chair. She ducked into it, pulling another chair over the hole she had just wedged herself into. The last thing she needed was to be seen. Once she was sure that she was completely hidden by the shadows, she forced her breathing to become silent and tried to hear above the sound of her heart pounding in her ears.

Chapter 5

Two Tommy gun noses came around the corner first and then two thugs right after them. They barely gave the barrier a second glance when they caught sight of the fire hose stretching around the doorframe and into the room that faced the street. They warily followed it into the semi-dark room, eyeing every shadow.

"Dey musta taken dah hose out dah window to dah ground," one noticed.

"Yeah," agreed the second, with a real scratchy voice "it's not like they could have gotten out any other way."

"Dey could be gettin' away. Dah longer we's stand here, the furthers away they's be gettin'. I's hopes you's ken drive fasta when you's be lookin' fors them's den you's did when's we's chasin' them's in dah car," the first voice jabbed.

"Ah, shud up. You're the one that can't work the gun," Scratchy informed as they came out of the room. They walked briskly down the hallway and started clanging down the metal stairs to the warehouse floor. The door reverberated shut, and a moment later a motor started out in the alley. Tires squealed for a split second, and then silence enveloped the warehouse again.

It wasn't until a moment or two later, when Olli tried to get out of her hiding spot, that she realized that she was stuck. The chair that she had managed to pull over the opening had now become the door to her small prison. *Aces! The perfect hiding place...now what?*

Dallas came out of a different room where he had hidden behind the door waiting for the thugs to leave. He looked around but didn't see his traveling partner. She didn't seem like the type to hide any longer than necessary. "Ma'am?" he asked the empty hallway.

Olli closed her eyes for a second. *How incredibly embarrassing.* "Ummm...I'm stuck." She rattled the chair that had trapped her.

Dallas looked at the barricade and his eyebrows rose. He didn't think that there was anywhere that she could have fit in. But then he saw her hands on the back of the chair, and that another chair had slipped down onto it, pinning it. He shifted the weight of the top chair and pulled the upside-down chair away from the opening. "There. Another chair had slipped onto it."

Olli watched the chair pull away and mentally braced herself for the teasing that was sure to come. She half-fell, half-crawled out of her hiding place and rolled to her feet. She looked up at him and smiled slightly. "Thank you."

Dallas turned the chair upright, set

it down and smiled crookedly at her. "Anytime. How did you fit in there?" he asked nodding to the crevice.

Olli looked over her shoulder at the fissure that she had managed to fit herself into and straightened her jacket. She looked back at Dallas and pursed her lips for a second. "I think it had something to do with the need for a place to hide." She grinned at him when the amused sparkle appeared in his eye. *It's nice to have someone around. Too bad I'll never work with him again. Why do I feel so much safer around him?*

"Where to now?" he asked. "A tour of the building and its surrounding area?" The sparkle still danced in his hazel eyes. He started down the hall with her.

Olli stopped halfway down the stairs and surveyed the empty warehouse floor. "As much as I would like to discuss square footage and decorating possibilities, I think this place is a little too gone for the effort. So we should probably start back." She looked at him over her shoulder and smirked. Her feet pounded out a rhythm on the metal steps as she half-skipped down them.

Dallas smiled to himself and walked with her across the empty floor. He stopped her with a hand motion when they were close to the door. All of his senses were on red alert while he slowly opened the door and checked the alley. When he was sure that it was empty, he opened the door and motioned her through. "I suppose now we have time for proper introductions. Detective Dallas Stowe, Ma'am."

Olli stopped and smiled. "Nice to meet you, Detective Stowe. District Detective Olivia Wainwright." She extended her hand to him, which he shook. "Call me Olli."

"I'm sorry I couldn't be more presentable, Miss Olivia," Dallas apologized, smudging the blood that had dripped from the cut above his eye as they started walking.

"When some of it is on my account?" Olli brushed it off. "How's your head feeling?" She didn't even really notice the fact that he had called Olivia. His accent enthralled her.

"It's had better days," Dallas obliged.

Olli nodded. She stole a sideways glance at him. It was nice to be able to walk next to him. Her romantic imagination could almost pretend that she was important to him. Which was complete nonsense. She made sure to be looking at the buildings when he glanced at her.

They walked in silence for a few moments. Each kept an eye out for a black car or two thugs to make sure that they weren't snuck up on and caught again.

"Where did all this come from?" Dallas asked, looking around at the buildings that towered over them. "I've lived here for a few months. People don't talk about this place. If they do it's with hushed tones. Why?"

Olli pushed her hands into her jacket's pockets. "Farther west is The Harbor. It's a really deep harbor. During the Great War Big Town was one of the busiest manufacturing cities once America joined the fight. And because of that a <u>lot</u> of money flowed into Big Town. Then when the war ended and the Twenties hit, people started building houses and better businesses on the edge of town. Pretty soon the entire town moved to the east. The only people who didn't leave were the thugs and Joey Leftfoot's crime family. A decade later, people are terrified of this place."

"I can understand that. Do ships not come into The Harbor anymore then?" Dallas looked back over his shoulder.

Olli bobbed her head side to side. "Not as often as they used to."

"Interestin'."

The first distant, muted rumble of thunder seemed to remind Olli of something. "Dallas, I uh…I just wanted to…" Olli gritted her teeth for a second. Why was it so hard to thank him? "I just wanted to thank you for what you did in the…in the car. With Ace."

Dallas smiled at her. "Anybody would have done the same thin'."

Olli shook her head. "I don't think so. Ace has a nasty reputation, and it really takes a special person to take him on when he has a gun pointed with the hammer back." Olli took a few more steps. "I just don't understand how I didn't get grazed somewhere." She glanced at Dallas, and a rip on his sleeve caught her eye. She stopped and focused on it.

Dallas took a few more steps and then looked back at Olli. "Miss Olivia, is something wrong?"

Olli pointed her right forefinger between her eyes and slowly turned it around so it was pointing at Dallas' arm. "That's why. It grazed <u>you</u>."

Dallas looked down to his arm, pulled his sleeve so he could see the rip a little better and frowned. "I liked this jacket," he grumbled.

Olli grinned and laughed slightly. "Let's get as far as we can before that storm gets over us," she suggested. It seemed best to let the subject drop for the moment. He looked almost embarrassed.

Dallas nodded, looking over his shoulder up at the swiftly darkening sky. He offered his arm to Olli, which she took with some hesitation, and they started off at a brisk walk.

"Need a ride?" Dee's voice asked in Olli's ear a few minutes later.

Olli stiffened for a second. She had forgotten about Dee. "It wouldn't hurt," she agreed dryly as another clap of thunder echoed closer over their heads.

"What wouldn't hurt?" Dallas looked down at her.

Olli paused with her lips pursed and a finger in the air then shook her head.

"Never mind. I'll explain later."

Dee's voice in her ear informed, "There should be a ride at the end of the alley."

At that moment, a jet black five-window coupe rolled to a stop at the far end the alley.

"Miss Olivia, we have company," Dallas announced warily, eyeing the coupe. He didn't trust the look of it.

A broad-shouldered, tall figure in a cowboy hat stepped out of the driver side, and walked around the nose of the coupe, a shotgun resting easily in the crook of his elbow. He leaned against the nearest front fender, his cowboy-booted right foot resting against the tire, shotgun leveled in the direction of Dallas and Olli.

Olli grinned. She knew who it was. After a quick glance at the clouds that were starting to roll over The District, Olli jogged toward the coupe. She just expected Dallas to come with her.

Dallas caught up to her and stopped her, his hand just above her elbow. "Miss Olivia-"

Olli interrupted. "Dallas, he's a good friend," she assured, looking at the cowboy. She un-hooked her elbow from his grip.

"With a shotgun?" Dallas didn't look convinced. So far he had no reason to doubt her, but it seemed a little strange that she would have friends in the middle of where they were.

"He's insurance just in case there

was another car that were to cut off our escape from that direction…" Olli paused when squealing tires interrupted her. She looked back and saw a black sedan. Her eyes widened slightly. "Like that…you're going to have to trust me." Olli flat-out ran toward the coupe when the front doors of the sedan started to swing open.

Dallas didn't like the way that things were going, but if Olli was positive that the cowboy and coupe were to be trusted, there was no arguing. He sprinted after her.

Two men stepped out of the sedan, bringing their Tommy guns with them. Gun fire echoed off the close buildings as lead was sent whistling toward the detectives.

Olli didn't stop running; she just dove through the open door of the coupe and rolled into the back seat. The cowboy fired the first round from his shotgun, slightly above the thugs at the other end of the alley. He wasn't there to kill anyone, he was just there as a driver.

Dallas was in a moment later, falling onto the empty front seat. He glanced back and watched the thugs duck as the cowboy's next round came a little lower. He reached out and slammed the door shut quickly.

"Hold that, will ya?" the cowboy requested, shoving the shotgun through the open window into Dallas' lap.
The cowboy ran around the nose of his

coupe and slid under the wheel, slamming the door as he quickly shifted the gears. "Afternoon, Oliver," he grinned at her.

Olli grinned back at him. "Dallas, let me take that, you're going to need your hands free." She held her hand over the backrest of the front seat, and then abruptly fell backward into the back seat as the back tires of the coupe squealed and smoke churned off them as it shot down the alley. It easily roared out of reach of the chattering Tommy gun fire.

Dallas shoved the gun back at her, puzzled when he saw the smirk on Olli's face.

Olli took the gun and eyed the two clips on the middle of the seat back. They were built specifically for the gun she was holding, but it was not an easy fit when one was attempting to place the gun in them while involved in a car chase. Her first attempt slammed her knuckles against the fabric. The next time, she smashed the stock of the gun against the right side of the cabin.

"Hey now, careful!" the cowboy protested.

Olli glanced at him, her lips pursed. She almost had it lined up and was just about to push the gun into the clips when the cowboy slammed on the brakes and took off quickly again, throwing her forward and then immediately into the backrest of the back seat. By now, her face was a mask of concentration.

"Yore aim a little off there, Oliver?" the cowboy asked conversationally as he whipped the coupe into a squealing, sliding left turn.

Olli looked up and narrowed her eyes. "What is it with you moonshiners and not being able to hold a straight line?" she demanded, giggling.

"If you don't want to get caught, the best way is avoidin' straight lines," the cowboy instructed like he was teaching a class.

"You could do it! I've seen you get away clean in a straight line," Olli grumbled, smirking as she missed the left clip and had to try again.

"Of course I can. It's jist not as much fun," the cowboy glanced back at her quickly, a teasing glint in his blue eyes. He easily slid the coupe into a narrow alley, the front right fender almost kissing a brick building.

Dallas braced himself up against the door and stiffened his neck quickly before his head cracked against the window. He looked at the two other occupants of the car like they were crazy. They had almost died at least four times that afternoon.

The sedan bounced off the building, but managed to keep up with the coupe. The cowboy quickly cranked the wheel to the left and slid the coupe into a wider, main alley. "What have I told you about sayin' goodbye to your friends?" he asked, glancing back at Olli.

Olli turned from watching out the back window. "I guess my friends have a hard time saying goodbye," she returned with mock sincerity.

The cowboy hat dipped as he nodded just as sincerely. "I see that."

Olli managed to keep a straight face until she saw Dallas' confused look. She snorted and grinned. "Monte, this is Dallas Stowe. Dallas, this is Montana Dirks. He's the fastest get-away driver in the state," Olli's voice had an unmistakable fondness in it.

Monte slid the coupe to a stop and backed into an alley and chuckled when the sedan roared by because it was going too fast to stop.

Olli quickly snapped the gun into the clips. "There!"

"What took you so long?" Monte demanded as he cut a course across the alley and headed perpendicular to the sedan.

"No thanks to you!" Olli complained.

"You need more practice," Monte told her, a huge grin on his face.

Olli stuck her tongue out at him, even though his back was to her.

"Don't you stick yore tongue out at me!" Monte pulled the car to the right.

Dallas looked between the two of them, wondering if they were ever going to take their escape seriously.

A surprised frown flashed across Monte's face as the sedan slid to a stop, from a cross alley; cutting them off, Tommy guns bristling from the driver's window and over the roof. "Oopsie." Monte slammed the wheel as far right as it would go and managed to convince the coupe to squeal into a cross alley just short of the sedan. A split second later the Tommy guns chattered after the coupe, spraying chucks of brick. A huge grin had come back onto Monte's face.

"That was a little close," Dallas muttered, slowly releasing his neck muscles that had kept him from cracking his head against the window.

"I heard that," Monte glanced at him quickly. "Relax. Enjoy the ride."

Dallas looked at him like he was insane and nearly slid off the seat as Monte slammed on the brakes to make a quick left turn.

The sedan managed to track the fleeing coupe down again. Once the sedan had locked on behind the coupe, a Tommy gun came out the passenger window, the shooter waiting for a clear shot, taking whatever he could.

Monte swerved as much as the alley would allow. "Shootin' guns. That's cheatin'," he grumbled. "Course, I suppose they need all the help they kin get drivin' a Buick sedan," he chuckled to himself.

Lightning flashed up in the sky, and thunder cracked down over the roofs of The District. Rain began to fall; large drops splattering against the windshields, kicking up mist from under the tires, causing the sedan back off from the coupe.

The rain didn't seem to even register with Monte. He seamlessly adapted to the slicker pavement and continued to drive just as before.

Olli, attempting to not slide across the entirety of the back seat, was watching out the windows not really registering the buildings flying by. A huge clap of thunder startled her and she suddenly recognized where they were. "Monte, you need to lose them now! If they follow us over The Line shooting, I'm going to catch it. I do not need a dead civilian on my hands!"

"But I was jist startin' to have fun!" Monte complained, grinning back at her.

"Monte, no dead civilians!" Olli looked through the back window as bullets spit from the nose of the Tommy gun.

"No dead civilians. Consider it done." Monte threw the coupe into a slide and cut into a different alley, pointing the nose toward The Harbor.

The driver of the Buick seemed thrown off for a moment. But he quickly adapted and followed after the coupe.

Dallas watched the conversation between the two other people in the car and braced against the door of the coupe. "How long have y'all known each other?" he questioned.

"Oh, quite a while." Monte cranked the wheel to the left and gritted his teeth as he helped his car make the turn. But he didn't stop with one left turn. He took the coupe around three more screeching turns.

Olli bounced off the backrest of the front seat when the coupe stopped just short of the alley they had been in only a minute before.

"Wha-?" Dallas started

Monte held up a finger cutting off the rest of Dallas' sentence. "Jist…wait." A split second after the sedan roared by, Monte had the coupe roaring across the alley and cutting around a couple more buildings.

When the coupe shot out of the side alley, Monte was only a few feet from the Buick's rear bumper. The coupe stayed solidly with the sedan, bobbing and weaving, sliding around corners and narrowly missing buildings.

Monte began to slowly inch up on the sedan, his eyes darting between the distance separating the two cars, the buildings flashing by, and the road ahead.

A Tommy gun's nose came out of the sedan's front window and started flashing back at the coupe.

"Hey now!" Monte snapped, cranking the wheel and pulling the coupe into a cross alley. "Hold on, Kids," he called. He took the car through a couple of quick, tight turns and brought it screeching and rocking back in behind the sedan.

Dallas barely had time to tighten up his forearm muscles to keep from sliding across the front seat into the crazy cowboy.

Olli sat up from falling against the right side of the coupe, reached over the backrest, and patted Monte's shoulder.

"Here we go," Monte hollered, shifting gears and slamming the accelerator to the floor.

The coupe roared forward, closing the gap quickly. Monte carefully guided the nose of the coupe toward the passenger side of the Buick. Just when the alley widened, the sedan's driver suddenly seemed to realize what was about to happen and tried to quickly turn left. Monte calmly eased the coupe along with the jerky defensive move by the Buick's driver, gaining ground.

The coupe's front bumper lightly kissed the right rear fender of the Buick, sending the sedan spinning out of control on the slick, wet pavement. The sedan headed nose first toward a set of concrete steps. Just before the car launched up the steps, the front doors opened and the two men rolled out, bouncing off the drenched pavement.

The Buick bounded up the steps, sparks and pieces of the undercarriage spraying out from under the car. The heavy sedan roared up the last few steps and crashed into the front of the sturdy brick building, spraying chunks of mortar and door.

The two men picked themselves up off the soggy road and watched the coupe

disappear in a trail of mist. Once they
were sure that they were both all right,
the two of them began to walk toward The
Line in a wary manner. Turning their
backs on The Harbor. They were on foot
in The District. Trusting things to be
safe and quiet until they got to The
Line was a bad idea.

Chapter 6

The black coupe fishtailed across The Line not soon after, Monte whooping and grinning from ear to ear. "Haven't had that much fun in a while!"

Olli smiled at Dallas. "I told you he was good."

Dallas shook his head. "Never seen anything like that."

"Course you haven't," Monte grinned over at him. "You jist met me!" They were getting into a more populated part of Big Town, slowing and weaving in and out of the traffic that was going the speed limit. "We're all set now, Oliver," Monte announced, easily weaving between two hacks. Then a siren alerted them to the fact that a policemen had noticed their reckless pace, following close behind despite the relentless sheet of spray that covered the windshield.

"Oh, yeah, we're home free now," Olli agreed, looking out the back window of the coupe. "Go ahead pull over and I'll take care of it." She wriggled up into the front seat as Monte slowed the coupe down to a nice stop. "'Scuse me, Dallas."

Dallas opened his door and stepped out into the rain. He closed the door behind her after she got out and waited with his arm resting on the roof of the coupe.

Olli started back toward the police car, but noticed that Dallas was still standing outside of the coupe. "Dallas? What are you doing?" she questioned, turning to face him.

"Waitin' for you to come back," he shrugged. There was really no point in attempting to stay dry.

Olli shrugged and turned back toward the police car. She stopped just shy of the officer between the two cars. "Officer," she nodded.

"Miss, I'm going to have to ask you to step into the car," the officer told her.

Olli's eyebrows rose. "Excuse me?"

"The hostage situation is over now. Step into the car." The officer nodded toward his car.

"What hostage situation?" Olli wondered, trying to decipher what this policeman was talking about.

"That would be you. That 'shine rig is obviously using you as leverage to get away clear." The officer nodded discreetly toward the black coupe.

"Officer..." Olli made a quick glance at his name tag. "Jackson. I'll take responsibility for the car, and I'm not a hostage. District Detective Olivia Wainwright." Olli reached into the inner pocket of her jacket and slipped out the wallet that had her badge pinned in it flipping it open so he could see it.

Officer Jackson took it and inspected it carefully. "I'll have to verify this, you understand."

Olli nodded. She didn't understand, but since she didn't have anything to hide, what was the point in arguing? "Control will verify it." Olli stood in the rain for a minute, not sure what to do as Officer Jackson stepped into his car and started to verify her badge number. She folded her arms and looked at the sky. It would have to be raining when a cop decided to check her badge. Why did he want to verify it anyway?

A more sheepish Officer Jackson stepped out of his rolling office and walked up to the meeting ground between the coupe and his car. "Here you are, Detective Wainwright. Sorry for the inconvenience. Try to keep the speed down in the future."

Olli took the wallet he handed her and slipped it into her inner pocket, warning bells going off in her head. Something didn't seem right, something besides the fact that the cop had wanted to check her badge. She smiled disarmingly, and nodded. "I'll see to it." Olli pretended to let her attention snap to something that moved behind Officer Jackson, and started backing away from him, watching his movements, ready bolt if he moved wrong. She stiffened for a second when a hand touched her shoulder.

JANELLE ARENS

"Everythin' all right, Miss Olivia?"
Dallas' southern accent asked quietly.

Olli nodded and turned toward him.
"I'll tell you in the car." She turned
and quickly walked toward the door of
the coupe, jerked it open and slid
across the front seat to the middle
seat, her shoulder almost pressing into
Monte's before Dallas could even move.

Dallas looked at the cop car for a
second, not sure what to do with the
situation he had just watched. He turned
and stepped into the coupe and closed
the door.

Olli sat between the two of them,
trying to figure out why she couldn't
unwind. She was still jumpy. Everything
looked a little out of place, and she
couldn't figure out why she couldn't
close the floodgates of her imagination.
She pulled her legs up and wrapped her
arms around her shins. Strange things
were happening, but it was nothing to
get worked up over she decided.

Monte waited until Dallas had swung
the door closed and slowly pulled away
from the curb, making sure not to call
any more attention to the black coupe.
"What's goin' on, Oliver?" he asked,
pushing his hat up a little and looking
at her.

"I don't know. It started when I got
to The District. Did you feel it, Monte?
The silence?" Olli rolled her neck and
looked at him for affirmation.

"Pin-drop silence. Yeah, I noticed.
Doesn't happen very often. Keep on your

80

toes." Monte nodded, easily gliding into a different lane.

"I plan to." Olli rested her chin on her knees. "Ace was at Two-Timer's today…" she started

Monte cut her off. "Somethin' ain't right. Those Ole Boys ain't looked at each other straight since the day Ace got here from the East,"

Olli nodded bumping her chin into her knees. "I <u>know</u>, and now that cop just checked my badge, and that's never happened before. What is going on?"

"He checked your badge?" Dallas entered into the conversation. Up until that point he had been observing the strange relationship she had with the cowboy. But, seeing Olli's exchange with the policeman had caught him wrong, too.

Olli nodded mutely. It was more like scrubbing her chin back and forth on her knees. There was so much to think about; what was going on? Her head was starting to feel like there wasn't enough room in it for all the thoughts that were bouncing around.

"Did he say that this was a runner?" Dallas asked.

Olli snickered a little, her eyes closing in mirth. "Yeah, he did. Not this coupe. A different one. This is Lightnin'," She couldn't help smiling at the tone in Dallas' voice. He obviously thought that she kept strange company. Not that she could blame him. "Monte bought her brand new a while ago. The only running she does is for me. No moonshine," Olli looked at Monte pointedly. "Right?"

Monte shook his head and looked at her like she had hurt him to his deepest feeling "It's true; I used to be the best 'Shine runner in the state." Monte's grin flashed. "That is, until I nearly ran down a twelve-year-old girl in the middle of the street." Monte slipped an arm around Olli's shoulders.

"It was clear when I looked." Olli shrugged when Dallas looked at her with his eyebrows raised. "I wasn't expecting a black coupe to come sliding around the corner and almost kill me."

Dallas nodded, unsure with what to do with the information. "May I see your badge, Miss Olivia?"

Olli looked at him. "Why?" She was instantly on her toes again. It wasn't that she meant to be suspicious, but strange things were happening.

"You say that he checked your badge and that it isn't normal. So I just wanted to see if it's been tampered with, that's all," Dallas explained.

Olli looked at him for a second and then nodded and worked her badge out of her inner pocket again and put it in his outstretched hand. "I don't think that you're going to find anything."

"You never know," Dallas shrugged, opening the wallet, and inspecting the badge. Then he turned the wallet over and looked at it for a moment. He closed it and handed it back to her with another shrug. "If I were you, Miss Olivia, I would take it to the lab and let them look at it."

"I'll most definitely be bringing it down for a check," Olli nodded, taking it carefully and sliding it into its place again. She completely agreed with Dallas. Hopefully nothing would come of it.

A moment later, Monte slid the coupe into a clear spot next to the sidewalk that lead up to WDA. "There ya are. Jist call anytime. I'll be there as fast as I can roll," Monte promised, looking down the line.

Dallas stepped out and let Olli out, closed the door and leaned on the open window frame. "It's a pleasure to meet such a good friend of Miss Olivia's. I don't think she was exaggeratin' when she said that you are the best."

Monte's hat brim dipped and he shrugged good-naturedly. "Just havin' fun."

Dallas dipped his head side to side with a little shrug, appreciating an ex-'shine runner's need for the chase, and his crooked smirk surfaced for a second. "Thanks for riskin' your life for her."

"Don't forget my paint job...tires...windows," Monte added with a slight smirk.

Dallas' eyebrows rose for a second and his smirk appeared. And then he was serious again. "I owe you one."

Monte shifted slightly and his hands tightened on the wheel for a moment.

"Well, Lightin' is gettin' wet. It's time to put 'er away and get back to work. It was nice to meet you." He leaned forward slightly and touched the brim of his hat. "'Till next time, Oliver."

"Thanks again, Monte!" she called after him as the coupe pulled away from the curb.

Dallas quickly stood up and watched him go trying to understand the comment the cowboy made.

Olli smiled after the coupe. She turned to Dallas. "He likes you,"

"Work?" Dallas puzzled.

Olli giggled a little at the look of sheer confusion on Dallas' face. "He drives a hack."

"Does he now," Dallas was even more surprised.

Olli closed her eyes and shook her head a little as she giggled again. "Can you see Monte sitting still for very long?"

Dallas nodded. "A valid point. Shall we get inside, Miss Olivia? It doesn't appear that this is going to let up." They started toward the building together.

The doors were at the top of a set of wide-swept, shallow concrete steps with shiny brass railings. The revolving doors themselves were brass and glass, and the five story cut-stone exterior was a dark grey, which was darker now because of the rain running down its sides. About ten feet above the doors

Wainwright Detective Agency hung in big, black block letters.

Through doors was the first floor where the lobby and main floor detectives worked. Under the lobby was the lab. The second floor detectives had a little more standing than the lobby detectives. The third floor was dedicated to Olli's office, a conference room, Alan's office, and his missing partner's office, which was still empty. Floor number four was a library of sorts. Every kind of information about any person, whether or not they were an upstanding citizen, was stored and filed away. The top floor held the three computers of the Control Tower. No one in Big Town knew about the computers. The lab tech had built them from scratch. The first two floors of detectives had the best typewriters money could buy, despite The Depression ravaging the country.

Olli trotted up the steps with Dallas and pushed through the revolving door to the right with him right behind her. As soon as they were two feet into the lobby, a voice came over the building intercom: "Detectives Wainwright and Stowe to The District Detective's office."

Chapter 7

Olli snorted and laughed a little to herself. "Coming, Dee. Coming," she informed in a sing-song voice.

"Dee?" Dallas questioned, following her through the busy lobby.

"My secretary. You'll meet her soon." Olli shrugged and started up the stairs two at a time.

"I see." Dallas nodded and followed. He got in line behind her when the stairs became a little crowded.

Olli breezed into her office followed closely by Dallas who closed the door behind him. Olli suddenly halted mid-stride and surveyed the scene before her.

Alan Wainwright was sitting behind Olli's desk, and Dee was standing at the far corner. Her right hand was resting on the desk, her left positioned on her hip. They were both smiling at the drenched detectives.

"Welcome back," Alan greeted.

"Thank you," Olli puzzled as she unzipped her jacket and smiled over her shoulder at Dallas when he slipped it off her shoulders and hung it on the coat stand for her, next to his. "We're using my office?" she questioned, tilting her head in curiosity.

Alan nodded. "Arnie has a bug, so we're going to change things up. Dee will have to take notes for us instead."

"Oh. All right. Tell him I hope he feels better soon." Olli grinned at her comment. Her father's holographic secretary was British, and she could just imagine his face and tone as he corrected her father, saying that he had a virus, not a bug. She claimed the second of the black leather chairs that faced her desk, the one closest to her floor length windows, and got a smile from Dee. She shifted uncomfortably. Her wet pants were sticking to her legs.

Dallas took the hint and sat in the other chair closest to the door, doing his best to not stare openly at the nearly see-through girl. He wished that he could look a little more presentable for the president and owner of the company, but there really wasn't much he could do about how wet he was at the moment.

"Where would you like us to start, Al?" Olli wondered, settling a little lower in her chair, resting her elbows on the armrests and folding her hands.

Alan leaned back a little and turned slightly so he was facing Dallas. "I think we'll start with you, Detective Stowe." He held out his hand, gesturing for Dallas to start.

Start Dallas did. He sat up a little straighter and almost looked over his shoulder before he caught himself and relaxed. "Mr. Wainwright, before we go any further, can I make a petition?"

Alan's eyebrows rose and he nodded. "Of course."

"Can you please call me Dallas, Sir? When you say Detective Stowe, I start looking around for my father," Dallas asked.

"I understand. My father was a detective before me. Dallas, you have the floor." Alan nodded in understanding and gestured for him to start his report.

"Thank you, Sir. One more thin'. What is that?" He nodded toward the girl.

Dee smiled at him good naturedly. "I'm a holograph, Dallas. Essentially a life size image. Which is why you can almost see through me. I'm Olli's secretary. It's nice to meet you."

Olli smirked at Dallas' confusion. "Al has one too. We don't usually let people see them simply because they're so hard to explain."

Dallas looked at her and slowly nodded. "I bet. Us normal people are still getting used to phones."

Olli smirked and shook her head. "Dee has a personality and can do anything a real secretary can. Except pick up anything solid."

Dallas looked at Dee one more time. "Interestin'. I received a call from the Control Tower sayin' there had been a break-in at 25 EW South and 1st Avenue, and that a detective was needed to assess the scene. There was a cab outside, which I directed to Last Street. I was then directed by the cabbie to EW South and 1st. Once I reached 1st, there were no police or police cars, and the store looked to be deserted completely and for a long while, too. There was a single black sedan parked across the street. It was then that I decided that it would be better for me to leave because something seemed wrong. I turned and walked three steps and was attacked from behind. A cloth soaked with chloroform was pressed over my face. And you were there when I woke up, Miss Olivia." He turned to Olli.

Olli was leaning on the left arm of her chair, staring off into space, her first two fingers propping up her chin. She was listening with one ear. She hadn't even heard her name. She was thinking about his first few sentences. It was weird that there was a called-in robbery in The District in the first place. And why would Dallas be sent on a strange call instead of her? And why was Ace at Two-Timer's headquarters in the first place? And the exploding silence…what was that all about? "Dee, can you see if you can find out why Ace was at Two-Timer's headquarters. And where he was before that." Olli suddenly realized that there were other people in the room. She started and straightened. "Oh, Dallas, I'm so sorry. Continue on." Olli pressed her hands together and turned to him, her eyes wide. "I was listening." She pointed both first fingers at Alan when she caught him opening his mouth out of the corner of her eye.

"Olli." Alan smiled at her.

"I promise I was," Olli nodded. She turned to Dallas. "I promise."

"Olli-" Alan started.

"Yes, Da-Al?" Olli caught herself and then looked between Dallas and Alan.

"We were waiting for you to tell your part of the story," Alan informed, barely containing a chuckle.

Olli's mouth opened slowly and she nodded. "Oh. I see. Sorry. I was here, reading a daily report-"

"Finally. It only took me five minutes to convince her this morning," Dee cut in.

Olli looked at her for a moment and cleared her throat. "And then you called me and informed me about the mix-up. I went down to 25 EW South. From there I went to Two-Timer's headquarters, where Ace caught me half-way down the stairs just above Two-Timer's office." Olli pulled a face, "I was then handcuffed to Dallas, and Ace and Two-Timer proceeded to argue over who was going to have custody. Ace whisked us away from Two-Timer and revealed a new tunnel in the floor of the warehouse. I think that's his main route for stealing Two-Timer's 'shine. We were shoved into a black sedan driven by one of Ace's drones and chased by a couple of Two-Timer's thugs. They shot at us quite a bit. Ace was thrilled about that—you know how he is. After a couple of minutes, we took evasive action." Olli struggled to regain a visage of professionalism when she saw her father fighting a grin. "Our combined efforts rendered Ace and the driver of our car unconscious. The car ran into one of the old buildings near The Heart, and we made our get-away on foot. Dee sent Montana, who picked us up at 21st and Alley 3 in Lightnin'. We were then chased and fired upon by an unknown black Buick sedan. We escaped only after Montana tapped the Buick into the concrete stairs going up to the office building on 1st Alley. We were pulled over just past Randall, the cop checked my badge...Dee-" Olli paused and shot a look at her secretary.

Dee nodded. "I'll check into it." She sat primly on the corner of the desk, her right leg hooked over her left, pad of paper and a pencil in her hands, taking notes.

"And I'll make a call to the department and double-check as soon as we're done here." Alan's face was dark. Olli knew that he was not pleased.

Olli glanced over Dallas, then focused on the clock over her door. "We arrived twenty-five minutes ago, and debriefed you and Dee," she finished, then leaned back against the chair and propped up her chin on the first two fingers of her left hand again.

"You two have had quite the adventure today. You will work together well, I believe. Dallas, go home, put some ice on your head, and get a good night's sleep." Alan smiled and nodded, dismissing him.

Dallas smiled back and nodded. "Thank you, Sir. I'll do that. Good night, Miss Olivia, Miss Dee, Sir." He stood and caught up his jacket just before he walked out the door.

"Good night, Dallas. I hope your head feels better soon," Olli barely was able to respond.

Dallas' crooked grin appeared for a moment, and then he closed the door.

It was quiet in The District Detective office for a moment. Alan leaned back in the chair and tented his fingers; Dee's pad and paper zapped out for a nail file, and she began to file her perfect nails while she waited for the silence to break.

Olli looked at the door for a moment, then she closed her eyes and turned to her father, her hands held up in a stopping motion, her eyes still closed. "What?" She slowly blinked her eyes open and looked at her father. She wasn't quite sure what had just happened, but she was sure that her father was making a mistake. *Dallas! Of all the detectives in the building...Dallas!* It wasn't that Dallas was a bad detective, Olli just couldn't figure out her emotions around him. He could make her feel completely incompetent one moment, and the next he made her feel like she could do anything.

"Dallas will be your partner from tomorrow on," Alan informed patiently. He had expected this.

Olli slowly nodded. "That's what I thought you said." She looked around the room for a moment, trying to formulate a protest, "But…Dad…I fly solo." She let her professionalism slide.

"Olli, you and I both know that you can't be two places at once. And you can't keep pulling Montana away from his hack job every time you need back-up. Not to mention you enjoy his company already," Alan explained a slight smile on his face.

Olli propped her elbows on the arms of her chair again and folded her hands under her chin. She thought about it. She had to admit, it was easier with him around. After all, if he hadn't been there today when she got stuck between the desk and chairs, how would she have gotten out? It was just going to be so strange to work with someone. She nodded, slowly agreeing with her father. "All right, Dad. I'll try for two weeks. Two weeks. And if I can't stand it, then I go back to working by myself."

Alan smiled and nodded. "Fair enough. But I must warn you, Olli, once you have a good partner, it's hard to go back to working alone." He stood up and walked around Olli's desk, and stopped long enough to rub her shoulders and kiss the top of her head. "Goodnight, Kitten. I'll see you at home." Just before he closed the door he looked at her one more time. "Make me proud." He smiled at her, the door clicked shut, and Olli and Dee were alone.

Dee turned so she was facing Olli a little more. "He's good-looking." She said, trying to sway Olli's thinking.

Olli sighed, stood, walked over to her windows, and looked out toward The District. "I sure hope Dad knows what he's doing. Me, have a partner? That seems strange." Olli turned to Dee.

Dee nodded. "He's your father. He has a good reason. Isn't he handsome, though?"

Olli's eyebrows rose. "Because that's important for being a good detective," she retorted, a scoffing tone creeping into her voice.

"I'm sure it doesn't hurt. You know you think he is. You just won't admit it." Dee got off Olli's desk and walked over toward her. "I promise, I won't tell anyone.

Olli decided to leave that comment hanging. "Well, I'm going to run down to the lab for a minute, just so Lenny can check my badge and make sure everything is kosher. I think I'm going to stay late and get some paperwork done." Olli started toward the door, stopping long enough to fish her badge out of the inner pocket of her jacket.

"I'll be here," Dee nodded. She looked pleased that Olli was going to stay and take care of the piles of papers that covered her desk.

Olli started down the stairs, smiling

to herself and nodding to the detectives on the second floor as she passed them. She slid down the banister to the first floor and headed across the lobby to the back of the building for the stairs to the lab.

"…You better think about it, Kid. We'll be back."

Olli stopped dead and glanced around. Her eyes locked on the partially open back door, and she carefully started toward it. She slipped stealthily through the door and looked first one way and then the other. It was still raining quite hard, but there wasn't anyone in the alley anymore. Whoever it was must have taken off toward Main Street where they could blend in with the crowds going home for the night. She trotted down the outside steps into the rain, not sure what she was looking for, but the curiosity of it all intrigued her. Olli walked down the alley a few feet toward Main Street, eyeing the shadows warily; the last thing she needed was to be jumped. She stopped and folded her arms. *Nothing.* Maybe she had just imagined the sound of a man's voice. *But that seems like quite a jump, even for me.* She looked up at the sky and frowned. The rain appeared to be staying for longer than predicted. A grunt startled her out of her weather side-track. Olli spun around on her heel and looked back the way she had come. A man was stumbling unsteadily to his feet by the back steps. Her eyes widened.

"Dallas?" She jogged back to him and touched his left arm. "Dallas, what happened to you?"

"Just fell down the stairs, Miss Olivia," he shrugged. There was a cut on his right cheek bone, and his left eye was going to be a yellowish-green color for a while, and the cut above his eye had started bleeding again. A new bruise on the left side of his chin, his bottom lip was split and a little puffy, and there was a short cut on the bridge of his nose, which was obviously broken.

Olli's eyebrows rose for a second. "If these steps got you that good, make sure you're careful around the stairs in the lobby, they're nasty." Olli smirked. "Broke my left leg on them once. It was embarrassing." She slid her hands on either side of Dallas' face.

Dallas looked at her for a moment, slightly distrustful. "What are you doin'?"

"Your nose is broken. This is going to hurt. On three ok?" Olli nodded slightly.

"All right." Dallas' jaw muscles clenched.

Olli took a steadying breath. "One," and pushed his nose hard to the left.

Dallas winced but only grunted slightly. "Is it straight?"

Olli pulled her hands back feeling a little unsure of herself now that she was finished straightening his nose. She nodded. "It looks normal again," she said in a way of explanation.

Dallas nodded. "I'll bet."

"I'm sorry. I know that hurts." Olli shifted uncomfortably.

"Not as bad as it did when it broke," Dallas gingerly touched his nose and winced.

"Don't do that. Let's get you back inside, out of this weather." Olli directed him toward the steps back inside WDA, while looking back down the alley toward Main Street. 'Who would pull a detective out of WDA and beat him up here?' She wondered.

They walked up the stairs in silence, smiling politely when they got close to someone. Once they walked through the door to Olli's office and closed it, Olli turned to Dallas and her eyebrows went up.

"All right, Dallas, what really happened?" she asked, pointing for him to sit in a chair.

Dallas eased himself out of his leather jacket and hung it on the back of the chair, then sat down. "Well, I was going to take a shortcut through the back alley to Main Street to avoid some of the crowd. As I was walkin' toward Main, a man in his mid-thirties cut off from the crowd and started down the alley toward me. I didn't think anythin' of it until he nodded. That's when I was grabbed from behind and realized a little too late that I was in over my head." Dallas went on to explain, to the best of his memory, about the fight. There wasn't much. He had been jumped and after a solid right, he was fighting fuzzy.

Olli pressed a slightly damp cloth to the cut above his eye listening to the tale. "Hold that there," she told him when he paused for breath. "So you got jumped from behind, again, beat up and told that you better think about it? What did they look like?" she asked rapid fire, searching his face.

Dee materialized behind her. "More importantly, are you feeling all right, Dallas?" she questioned sitting on the desk to Olli's left.

Dallas and Olli both looked at her for a second, and Dallas smiled slightly. "I'm fine, thank you, Miss Dee. Yes, to your first question, Miss Olivia. Your second question…" Dallas paused to think for a moment. "The first man was 'bout my height. The second one…" Dallas frowned and shook his head. "I really didn't get a straight look at him. It happened too fast."

Olli took the cloth from him and started dabbing at some of the blood that had slid down his face again.

"That's not much I know, but-" Dallas started.

Olli smiled at him. "It's all right, Dallas." She turned his chin so she could check out the bruise that was smeared across the bottom part of his jaw. "That's going to hurt for a day or two."

Dallas shrugged. "At least I taught them a lesson," he muttered wincing a little when the cloth bumped his bottom lip.

"Sorry." Olli's left eyebrow tipped down. "And what was that exactly?" she wondered, a giggle barely hidden in her voice.

"They learned that I'm not someone that they can scare easily, after all. I fought back." Dallas' hazel eyes sparkled with mirth.

Olli barely held back a snort and looked at him with a straight face. "So that beating was….unimportant?" She could hardly believe that she had been able to keep a straight face the entire time.

The cut rose with Dallas' eyebrows. "I got in a few good pokes, Miss Olivia. It wasn't a total loss," he defended, pretending to look hurt.

Olli nodded. "Indeed. All right, that's the best I can do with this. Want a mirror for the way home?" She tried to sound serious, but failed.

His eyes sparkled as he rose. "Why? Got one on you?"

"You can have the mirror by the door, but it might be a little unwieldy." Olli shrugged, nodding to the tall thin mirror between the door and the coat stand.

"I think it would be more of a hindrance than a help. But I'll keep it mind." Dallas smirked. He stood up, pulled his jacket off the back of the chair and draped it over his arm. "I'll see you in the morning, Miss Olivia." He nodded toward Dee. "Good night," he wished as he closed the door behind him.

Olli shook her head and couldn't help a slight smile. "All right." She sighed. "I'm going to try to make it all the way down to the lab and hand off my badge to Lenny. Hopefully, no one else is going to be in need of a patch job." She stood and started for the door.

Dee snorted. "You enjoyed every minute of that, Boss. Don't even try to deny it."

Olli paused with her hand on the door knob. She turned around and looked at Dee for a moment. Her lips pursed, and then she shrugged. "I'll be back." Olli pulled the door open and started down the stairs again. She hummed to herself as she half trotted, half-skipped down the broad steps. She walked easily across the polished, now-deserted lobby. She opened the door to the basement but not before checking to make sure that there wasn't anyone in the alley.

Chapter 8

The lab looked like a cutting-edge scientific lab. Even though there wasn't any scientific research coming out of WDA's basement, Lenny, the resident technician, was dedicated to doing everything he could possibly do to keep the detectives safe and in the know. If anyone could find if something had indeed happened to Olli's badge, Lenny was her best bet. Olli strolled up to the lab and knocked on the door frame. "Lenny, you in?" she called, glancing around the stark, white room. Searching for Lenny was like looking for a needle in a haystack. Lenny had unusual white hair and always wore a white lab coat over a white button up shirt. He was almost white himself, no matter how much time he spent outside. The only thing that kept him from completely melting into the backdrop of the room was his perfectly pressed black slacks that, somehow, never got anything white on them.

"Olli! Good to see you!" Lenny's white, Einstein-like hair, wide eyes and ageless, angled face popped up above the middle of a lab table not far away. He focused on one of the tubes, eyes almost crossed for a moment, and then unfolded his tall frame and stood upright.

"I'm glad you decided to stay a little late tonight. I think I might just have a challenge for you," Olli informed him, walking into the room without being invited. Test tubes and small glass beakers glowed almost eerily in the dusky half-light that lit the lab.

Lenny rubbed his hands together for a moment and then turned his chin a little to the right and his eyebrows rose, "What sort of challenge?" he wondered, eyeing the one detective for whom he did the least amount of work.

"Can you run some tests on this to see if it was tampered with? My partner and I think so, but I wanted to be sure." Olli held out the wallet with her badge in it and waited for Lenny to take it from her.

"Your badge? What would give you such an idea?" Lenny flipped the wallet open and then looked back at Olli, his eyes narrowing while waiting for an answer.

"Just take a look at it when you have some time, will you, Lenny? You know, if you turned on some lights, it would be easier to see what you were doing," Olli hinted, as she slowly meandered over to the far wall and flipped a couple of switches on. Two brilliant flashes later, the lab was bathed in a bright, clean light that lit the room to the darkest corners.

"No!" Lenny waved his arms back and forth nearly knocking Olli and test tubes over as he raced to the switches; turning the lights down quickly to level it was at before. "I'm working with a compound that is extremely sensitive to light. If the lights stay on too long, it'll blow!" He gestured with his hands, nearly hitting a low-hanging light, and quickly walked back to the tubes he had been working with when Olli walked into the room. After a quick glance at the tubes and gauges, he held up Olli's badge and smiled at her. "I'll take a look at it right away. You'll know as soon after I do if anything has happened to your badge."

Olli grinned at him in return, a fond look in her eyes. "I'll be in my office for a few hours, so if you come up with anything, you can look for me up there. Good luck." With that and a goodbye smile, Olli breezed out of the room and started the trek back up to her office.

Lenny waved with one hand, still eyeing the gauges distrustfully. After a few minutes, when he felt that things were stabilized enough that he could look away from the gauges, he gazed at the badge that was still wedged tightly in his right hand.

Dee materialized when Olli walked through her office door. "This is Goodnight, then?" she wondered, her head cocking slightly to the right.

Olli walked around Dee, skirted the

corner of her desk, and plopped down into her chair with as little grace as she could possibly muster. "No, Lenny's running some tests on my badge; I think something might really have happened. Besides, I already told you that I wanted to get some paperwork done." Olli smirked at Dee. If there was one thing that Dee would let Olli stay at the office late for, it was paperwork. Not that Dee could technically push Olli around, but she could be extremely bossy and annoying. If Olli stayed too late, without a very good reason, Dee would bother and badger her into going home and sleeping in her bed like a normal person.

Dee nodded in satisfaction. "Sounds like a good plan, Boss."

The two of them soon were slogging through daily reports. About two hours later, a knock interrupted the intense study of a map of a crime scene on Olli's computer wall.

Olli didn't turn from the map right away. "It's open," she called toward the door and then turned to see who was knocking.

Lenny bustled in with the wallet in his hand. A wide grin was almost splitting his timeless face in two. He looked as though he had made a breakthrough in how fast he had discovered something.

"Lenny! I didn't expect you for a while longer. Your best work yet, I do believe. What can you tell me?" Olli smiled brightly when she saw the satisfied grin on Lenny's face. She turned from the computer screen and sat down on the arm of the nearest chair.

Lenny held out her badge and began walking around in small circles after she took it, gesturing with his hands. "Your badge had a very fine residue from a new kind clay-like substance that makes an exact replica of whatever it is pressed over." He stopped for a moment. "I took the liberty of breaking down the compound and deciphering how to make it. This new clay will really come in handy at crime scenes. That's what took me so long."

"Had?" Olli asked, not missing the past tense. She flipped open the wallet and looked at her badge. He must have cleaned it, but it looked no different now than it had when she had walked it down to Lenny's lab in the first place. But that was the reason Olli was up in her office reading papers and keeping Big Town safe from The District and Lenny was down in his basement dwelling investigating things that were sometimes too small or too fast-working to see with the human eye. Then she remembered about the clay he was jabbering about. "Absolutely, anything you can do to make our lives a little easier," she conceded. She looked at the clock on the wall. *Two hours, and he thought that was long?*

Lenny nodded in exuberance. "I've never seen the compound before, so I cleaned it all off your badge so I could better study it. From what I can tell so far, the clay is fast-acting and forms a copy of whatever it is placed over in a matter of seconds. So the user could easily borrow something, like your badge, and make more than one imprint if so desired. I don't know if this helps you or not, but that is what I found out." For a split second his voice took on an anxious note. He was always up for helping a detective in WDA, but one of his worst fears was letting one down.

"I'm sure it helps. I'm just not sure with what." Olli stood and looked at her badge for a moment, unsure what exactly she was supposed to do with the information she had just been given. It had to have a place and a reason for being in the puzzle; Olli just wasn't certain what it was yet. She placed a hand on Lenny's arm. "Thank you so much for burning some midnight oil and taking a look at this for me tonight. Take the day off tomorrow. You deserve it."

Lenny's face split into a huge grin and he nodded. "Thank you, Olli, but I can't. See this clay residue that I broke down… I want to get started making a sample. See you next time, then." With that Lenny bustled out of the office and headed down the hallway toward the stairs.

"Suit yourself." Olli looked down at her badge and shrugged. She turned to Dee, who was sitting on Olli's desk, her legs crossed, waiting to continue. "Does two hours seem like a long time to you?"

Dee changed legs and smoothed her skirt. "I'm not the one to ask, Boss," she pointed out.

Olli knew that was a good point, and slipped her badge back into the inside pocket of her leather jacket. "Now, about this crime scene…"

It wasn't until about three in the morning that sleep finally snuck up on Olli successfully. Her eyes started closing heavily and barely blinking open at the last second. She nearly fell off her chair once because of the size of the jerk that ensued when she started awake. Olli shifted again, re-crossed her ankles on the desk, and focused on the daily report, set on finishing it before she fell asleep.

Dee popped into view about five minutes later, geared up to insist that Olli should go home for the night. She looked around the desk just in time to see the daily report that Olli had been reading fall out of her hand and drift to the floor. Dee walked around the desk and smiled at her. She didn't understand how Olli could just drift off to sleep in that position. "Pleasant dreams, Boss." Dee smiled fondly. She disappeared, and the lights blinked off.

Olli stood in the middle of the foggy, damp cemetery. She looked around, eyeing the fog, not trusting it, not quite sure how she got there. While she watched, a headstone suddenly came up in front of her. Without meaning to, Olli looked at it. Martha Wainwright, *Dearly Loved and Missed*, and the dates of her birth and death were carved into its flat, damp surface. Olli dropped to her knees in front of the headstone, covering the bottom half of her face with her hands, doing her absolute best not to cry. Suddenly the scene changed and Olli was now standing on the front steps of WDA, but it was years previous. Olli looked at the street and saw three police cars and six policemen, commanded by her young uncle, pulled across the road in a stand-off with thugs holding Tommy guns, leaning across their black sedans. Olli's eyes snapped down the street to her right. A younger Olli ran from a civilian car with her hand tightly gripping her mother's. Olli tried to tell them to go back, turn around, leave before anything happened, but no sound came out of her mouth. A burst of gunfire echoed down Main Street, and Olli turned in time to see her uncle fall, bright blood slowly seeping down the front of his smart blue uniform. She looked back over to her younger self and her mother. Olli watched in horror as her mother sent her toward the front doors, and ran off toward the stand-off, calling her brother's name. Olli looked to the back door of the closest black sedan and watched as the door swung open. Out stepped a burly man, and a Tommy gun seemed to be part of him. Olli looked frantically between him and her mother.

No, this couldn't be happening! Not again! The Tommy gun swung up and a deadly spray of lead covered her mother's back. Olli looked over at her younger self in time to see her start toward the street only to be caught before she could go two steps by Jake, her father's partner, who picked her up and swooped her inside. Olli looked back at her mother, who was lying in the street, her blood pooling around her. She was about to head toward her mother herself, when a laugh stopped her dead in her tracks and sent shivers up her spine. It was Ace.

Olli sat bolt upright, drenched in a cold sweat, breathing heavily. She looked around groggily, trying to figure out where she was. But the scan of her surroundings stopped instantly when she made out Ace standing in front of her, a wicked smile on his face and his handgun pointed directly between her eyes. Olli didn't wait a second longer. She lashed out, slapping his arm away and adding a straight-arm blow to his chest sending him reeling backward. She quickly followed with a lunge and a hard left to his midsection, which he caught in his chunky fist. Her open-handed blow to his face with her other hand was blocked by a shackling grip on her wrist. A deft move spun her around, her arms imprisoned by his. She took a deep breath, shaking slightly and breathing raggedly, but ready to start round two. Suddenly she caught their reflection in the mirror by the door. She froze. Her eyes snapped wide. "Dallas?…I'm so sorry!…I didn't mean…I thought…I mean…" Dallas released her slowly and Olli plopped down in her chair and dropped her forehead on her fingertips, sighing in agitation.

"I had that nightmare again," she started through clenched teeth. "I'm standing out front of WDA ten years ago, watching Ace gun down my mom in cold blood. Then he laughed…" Her fist slammed down on the desk, startling Dallas. "He laughed! Like it was some sort of joke. First my uncle , then my mom. Arrgh!" she growled. She leaped to her feet and powered to the windows. "I'm not going to let him get away with it. Some day he's going to make a mistake, and I'm going to be there with the handcuffs." Olli pointed back at Dallas before tightly folding her arms over her stomach.

Dallas absorbed what she said, understanding now her animosity toward Ace. For a moment, he just looked at her consideringly. He walked up to the floor-length windows that faced The District and stood solidly next to her. He folded his arms and looked across Big Town toward The Harbor. "And you'll do it the right way, and he'll never breathe free air again."

It was quiet for a moment.

Olli watched the early morning sun peek over the buildings of The District. She pursed her lips and swallowed. "I thought you were Ace, coming toward me with that handgun of his pointed between my eyes."

Dallas glanced at her, nodded silently. "I was tryin' to wake you up I said your name a couple times, but you didn't answer. I was just goin' to touch your shoulder."

Olli took a deep breath and held it for a minute, looking out over Big Town. She slowly let the air out between her teeth and smiled apologetically at Dallas. "Sorry about that."

Dallas shrugged, and slid his hands into his pockets. "You were just reactin' to your surroundin's. I can understand that."

Olli's smile flashed. "Enough about my dreams. So, Dallas, let's summarize the last twenty-four hours of your life," she intoned, something bordering on amusement in her voice.

Dallas shrugged. "Well, my daily report is certainly goin' to be a little longer than usual, and a little more interesting to read, too."

"I'll say," Olli agreed. "Sent out on a bogus call, knocked out, come-to in Two-Timer's office handcuffed to a girl, pushed down the stairs and through a fox hole, all the while being shot at. Shoved into a car chase punctuated by Tommy gun fire, you managed to survive a head-on collision with a brick wall, outwit a pair of thugs on foot, and ended up in another car chase. Less than an hour later, you were beat up in the back alley for no reason at all. And just now, your new partner tries to cause you bodily harm. And you're here at quarter after eight because…?" Olli asked, glancing at the clock over her door.

"How could I stay away?" he asked. His hazel eyes searched hers out and held them for a moment until she blinked and looked down.

Olli felt like every hair on the back of her neck stood upright for a moment. She cleared her throat. "You need coffee? I feel like I could use something to wake me up."

Dallas nodded. The corner of his eyes crinkled up and mischievous amusement danced across his face for a moment. "After you, Miss Olivia."

Chapter 9

Coffee in hand, the two detectives were soon back in the office. Dallas was sitting on the arm of the chair closest to the windows, and Olli was sitting on her desk.

Dallas took a sip of his coffee and looked over at Olli. "So, if this were a normal day in the life of Olivia Wainwright, what would you be doing right now?"

Olli glanced at him and blew on her coffee; she had already burned the tip of her tongue. "If it were today in my life, I would still be sleeping,"

Dallas raised his eyebrows. "Because that was goin' so well for you this mornin'."

Olli took a breath like she was going to say something, changed her mind halfway through and blew on her coffee instead.

Dallas grinned, eyes hazel eyes sparkling.

"Good morning." Olli wished to the room over the edge of her mug just before she took a sip. The wall across from Olli slid silently open, and a printed message wished her good morning. Soon the screen blinked and a beautiful sunrise over The Harbor lit up the wall.

~~Dallas turned in time to see the last~~ part of the wall disappear into itself. He hadn't seen anything like it before. His eyebrows rose at the picture that appeared. He stood up and stepped around the chair. After glancing over the wall, he looked at Olli, ready for the explanation.

Olli smiled at him when he looked at her. "Neat isn't it?" she wondered, smirking over her coffee at him.

Dallas looked at it again and nodded. "Impressive," he agreed.

"There's more." Olli smiled. She turned back to her computer. "The morning news, please."

The screen changed color and became the front page of the morning news paper.

"No!" Olli whispered hoarsely, slowly set down her cup and stood up, staring at the screen in amazed horror.

Dallas looked at it, and he frowned. **BIG TOWN BANK CLEANED OUT! NOTHING LEFT! BIGGEST HEIST IN CITY HISTORY!** Screamed across the top of the page.

"It can't be!" Olli exclaimed walking around her desk and standing in front of the screen.

Dallas leaned against the back of one of the chairs. "It happens to every bank at one time or another, Miss Olivia," He pointed out.

Olli glanced at him and then back at the page. "You don't understand, Dallas. Our bank has the most high-tech security system in the state."

"How so?" Dallas asked, turning from the front page to her.

"There are entry codes on every door and drawer. Every half hour, the codes randomly change. If someone enters a wrong code, or forces a door, the police get a message. It does not appear that they got one. The night guard has the codes for the doors, but that's it. Al, Mayor Anderson and Ben Sandy, the bank owner, have all the codes and the time changes for each night." Olli sat on her desk and looked at the computer, a shocked frown frozen on her face.

Dallas folded his arms and smirked to himself. "Can we see the rest of the story, please?" he directed to the computer, feeling slightly foolish for talking to a wall.

The page turned and revealed the rest of the story and drawings of two suspects.

Olli was going to keep reading, but when she caught Dallas' start and tense shoulders, she looked at him. "What?" she asked.

"I'm not quite sure, Miss Olivia. I feel like I've seen them somewhere before." He rubbed the back of his neck, trying to figure it out.

Olli's eyebrows rose, and she pointed to the two black and white sketches with her right forefinger. "Where?"

"Well, I don't know for sure," Dallas side-stepped.

Olli looked closer at the drawings.

The one in the left picture was a handsome man who looked to be in his mid to late thirties. If she had to describe him, she would have called him a confidence man. He looked like the type to sneak his way into a deal if he could work it. The man in the right sketch was about ten years older and had a square jaw. He looked like he had seen and been in his share of fights, and he didn't look like he would lose easily. "The one on the right looks like the type that could really mess you up," she pointed out, folding her arms.

Dallas nodded in agreement.

"Something about this whole clean sweep of the bank bothers me. There's no way that they are the masterminds behind it." Olli took a bigger sip of her coffee.

Dallas studied the pictures again. The man on the right looked like a planner, but he didn't seem like the kind to plan a bank robbery of a bank with that kind of high-tech security system. "You're thinkin' it's an inside job, Miss Olivia?"

Olli nodded, her eyes narrowed. "That confidence man might have a trick or two up his sleeve, but there's no way that he's pushing that one on the right around. They definitely were pulling the job for someone." Olli pursed her lips for a second. "There's one good way to find out."

Dallas looked at her for a moment. "So I take it that our next stop is the bank itself?"

"That it is. Good morning, Dee," Olli wished toward the room in general.

Dee blinked into the room sitting on the desk, her right leg crossed over her left, and smiled over the rim of her coffee cup. "Good morning, Olli, Dallas," she wished.

"Good mornin', Miss Dee," Dallas acknowledged.

"Dee, could you make sure that movers get Dallas' things up here sometime today, the earlier the better, and make sure that the engraver gets the plates up on the door by the end of the day, too, if he can? We're going to swing by the bank and see what there is to see," Olli informed, slipping into her jacket when Dallas held it up for her.

Dee nodded. "I'll make sure it gets done. Happy hunting." She disappeared.

Olli nodded and started out of the room.

Dallas was about to follow her out when Dee popped up in front of him.

"Dallas, keep an eye on her. After she's had one of her nightmares, Olli tends to get a little…well…black and white. Try to keep her out of too much trouble," Dee informed, checking out the door to make sure that Olli didn't come back wondering what was going on and why Dallas wasn't following her.

Dallas slowly nodded. "Don't worry, Miss Dee, I'll see to it."

Dee nodded in satisfaction and then disappeared again.

Dallas walked out the door, leaving it open, side-stepped a pair of secretaries, and started down the stairs. He caught up with Olli about halfway down the flight.

Olli was leaning against the wall, her arms folded, waiting for Dallas to come down the stairs. When he started came close, she stood straight and smiled slightly. "Dee gave you the 'nightmare speech', didn't she? Again, I'm really sorry that I attacked you."

Dallas shrugged, and they started down the stairs together. "Everyone has a nightmare now and then. Don't mention it, Miss Olivia, really, it was nothin'."

Olli smiled a little to herself. It was nice that he was so forgiving. "Dallas, please call me Olli. I'd appreciate it."

Dallas conceded with a slight nod. "So what do you think of this entire bank robbery as a whole?" Dallas asked, skirting a young woman in a dress-suit who was walking up the stairs.

"We know what I think. What about you, Dallas? You've done nothing but agree with my observations since we started," Olli pointed out, watching the woman go up the stairs. Something seemed a little off with her. She had watched Dallas a little too long, or maybe it was Olli she had stared at, but it just seemed strange.

"The police are being sent off on a wild goose chase lookin' for them. These two are in the papers and in the public eye so that the real mastermind behind it all can slip away unnoticed." Dallas shrugged his eyes narrowed in thought.

They wound their way through the main lobby and Olli nodded in agreement. "It does appear that way."

Dallas followed Olli through the revolving door, and they pushed it around and stepped out into the early morning together. They walked toward the street, where cars and hacks of every color were driving back and forth. Dallas was about to hail a hack when Olli slipped her hand into his and squeezed it.

Dallas looked down at her, not sure what to do with the sudden contact. She was smiling like she was incredibly happy to be with him. Before he could recover from the contact enough to look at her strangely, she pulled to a stop, grabbed his other hand, and pulled him to face her.

Olli went up on tip-toe, using his hands for balance. "Dallas, go with it," she whispered, making it look like she was talking to him about something that would be frowned upon to talk about in public.

Dallas smirked for a second, then leaned her way a little.

"See that bruiser over by the clock shop?" Olli asked, covertly looking around to make sure that no one was close enough to hear what she was saying.

Dallas looked beyond the pedestrians walking past with newspapers and umbrellas left over from the light rain earlier that morning. He covertly studied the man across the street, who was leaning against the corner of the shop. He had his dark fedora pulled low over his eyes, was smoking a cigarette, and had a dark coat on. He stood in the shadows of the alley, appearing to be leisurely watching the passersby. "How long has he been there?" Dallas asked, leaning down so his cheek was almost touching Olli's.

Olli pulled back slightly and smiled shyly. "He came out about the same time we walked down the steps. I don't think that it was an accident." She leaned in close to him again. "What do you think?"

Dallas glanced over at him again. "I think he isn't falling for our show, Miss Olivia, and that we should be on our way before people start getting hurt." Dallas' eyes sparkled mischievously and he pulled her right hand up and easily kissed her knuckles.

Olli nearly fell over and blushed. She wasn't ready for something like that to happen. Her more sensible half plowed through and over her more romantically inclined thoughts, telling herself it was all part of the act. She glanced at a group of men and women that were heading past them, between them and the street. She took a quick look at the street. A lot of cars were coming and going suddenly, so if they were going to slip away, now would be the time to do it. "Dallas, walk with this group."

They quickly let go of each other's hands and slipped into the group at two different points. It wasn't until they were down the street and around the corner that they joined back up and started looking for a hack.

Olli looked up at Dallas. "You probably shouldn't do that again, Dallas."

Dallas glanced at her and then back at the crowd waiting for a hack. "Do what, Miss Olivia?"

"Kiss my hand like that. After all, you don't know where my hands have been," Olli informed him. She was slowly starting to get over the embarrassment now.

"That's not true, Miss Olivia. They've been with you your whole life," Dallas countered, like it was the most obvious thing.

Olli rolled her eyes and sighed a little. "You don't ever quit, do you?"

Dallas looked at her innocently. "I sure hope you're not in too much of a hurry to get to the bank, Miss Olivia. It might take a while with this crowd."

Olli surveyed the crowd for a moment, and then shook her head. "I don't think so." She walked to the corner, without making sure that Dallas was following, and after looking down the street, she stepped out into the lane a couple of feet.

A bright yellow hack with black and

white checkers going down the side
pulled up, slowing to a perfect halt in
front of her, just shy of her toes.

Olli looked back at Dallas as he
walked up and grinned. "He never fails."
With that, she opened the back door and
got in.

Dallas shook his head and got in
behind her. He closed the door and
looked into the front seat, not too
surprised to see the cowboy hat and
smirky grin that belonged to Monte.

"Good mornin'. We're headin' to the
bank I assume," Monte flung into the
rear view mirror as he pulled off into
the main stream of traffic again.

Olli nodded. "That would be great.
Just as close as you can get."

"I'll do my best, Oliver, but I don't
think I can drop y'all off at the steps,
if that's all right?" Monte's eyes
sparkled in mirth.

Olli nodded in understanding.

"Thank you for the offer, though,"
Dallas smirked.

Monte grinned at them and pulled off
the main street and cut into an alley
that would take them toward the bank.

"What's the word on the street about
last night?" Olli leaned forward
excitedly.

Monte's eyes flicked up to the mirror
for a moment, and then went back to
watching the road. "Well, lesse. It was
an inside job, and the two fellers that
robbed your fine bank were let in by
someone who was awaitin' for them

inside. That somebody's still a mystery."

Olli cocked her head and looked at Dallas out of the corner of her eye. "Anything else?"

"There is." Monte cut out of the alley and slipped between hack and a slow-moving sedan. "They made two trips in order to get all the money out."

Chapter 10

"Twice?!" Olli squealed. "How is that possible? How did they not set off the alarms?"

Monte nodded. "Some folk think that it was Ole Ben Sandy who did it, lettin' 'em in and all. There's others who think that he's too straight to be robbin' hisself." They turned off the road and onto another alley.

"He'd have to be in two places at once. He was in Eminences last night. There's no way that he could have gotten back in time to let those two in," Olli declined the idea.

Dallas looked at her and tipped an eyebrow.

Olli shrugged. "Ben Sandy's the owner of the bank, and a good friend of my dad. We basically know where he is all the time, not just because he tells us, either."

"For possible kidnappin' threats..." Dallas' voice trailed off.

"Or in case the bank gets robbed." Olli shook her head; she was still trying to figure out how it could have happened.

Dee's voice suddenly sounded in Olli's left ear. "He stopped in by your father this morning at six o'clock, quite distraught I might add, at the thought of half the town assuming that he had cleaned out their life savings for himself. It took your father almost an hour to calm him down." Dee mused. "You might want to check out the night watchman. It's a well known fact that they don't make much money, and Ben just hired a new man about three days ago. He had to because Toby Jenkins was shot outside the Blinking Lights," Dee informed.

Olli blinked. "Toby Jenkins was shot almost four days ago? How is it I wasn't informed of that?"

"You were in South Town with your father. When you came back, you had other responsibilities that were important, and the information went unannounced," Dee said apologetically.

Olli nodded, her lips pursed in thought. That did seem to make sense. Toby Jenkins would have never opened the door to anyone after hours unless they were with Ben, or they had his special permission to be there.

"Toby Jenkins?" Dallas inquired, entering the conversation for the first time. He would have said something sooner, but it was intriguing to him to watch Olli and Dee's relationship at work.

"He was the night guard at the bank. And had been for about six years. He was shot outside The Blinking Lights. It's a saloon owned by Razor. Rough place. All the locals go there to do their drinking. There's always someone who doesn't come home after a rowdy weekend." Olli shook her head. "Toby never tried to get promoted or make more money for himself. He was quite satisfied with where he was. Toby was a real level-headed man; I don't understand how he could have been in any part of any fight that started at the Lights. Hmm, we might need to stop there before lunch," Olli muttered. "I have a contact there," she informed when Dallas shot a puzzled look her way.

"Of course," Dallas nodded. That should have been obvious. Why wouldn't she have someone there watching when she was unable to?

The rest of the short trip was made in silence. Dallas watched out the window as the buildings flew past, Monte drove, and Olli pondered. It seemed that everything was happening at once. Toby Jenkins shot dead outside The Blinking Lights, a new watchman hired two days before the robbery, the two men robbing the bank which they cleaned out in two trips. Ace at Two-Timer's…there were too many questions without enough answers to go around. The whole situation was making her head hurt.

"This seems to be the end of the road, Detectives," Monte announced, breaking into Olli's thoughts.

A stern-faced cop was waving Monte

away from the barricade that had been set up. It did appear that there wasn't any way to get past it.

"Thanks again, Monte." Olli smiled at him as she slid out of the back seat and stood behind Dallas.

"I'll be waiting behind the hardware store for y'all." Monte nodded and waved toward the cop as he pulled away.

Olli looked at Dallas and they started toward the barricade of two cop cars across the road, half a dozen policemen to stop the traffic, and pedestrians that were going in the direction of the bank.

"You would think that the bank might be blown up at any second," Dallas muttered just loud enough for Olli to hear.

Olli shrugged. She was too busy looking at the unfamiliar policemen. Where did they come from? And why were they here?

Dallas and Olli weren't stopped almost instantly because they were walking with some authority and didn't look curious. It was only after they had slipped past the cop cars that they were stopped by the policemen on the other side.

An especially burly cop stepped in front of Olli. "I'm sorry, Miss, this entire block is off limits to civilians. I'm going to have to ask you to get back behind the barrier and go on your way." He eyed her leather jacket, knee high black boots tied over her pants and stared at her disapprovingly.

Olli smiled disarmingly. "I'm sure you heard it before, but I'm not a civilian. And this _is_ on my way." She pointed in the direction of the bank.

"You're right, Miss, I have indeed heard it before this morning. What are you? The manager at the bank? The owner's daughter? A detective at WDA?" The last question had a scoffing tone. "You can leave now," he informed her, reaching for her arm.

Olli swung her arm out of the way. She didn't appreciate the tone, but her smile stayed. "I _am_ from WDA, how'd you guess?" she asked cheerily, dodging another swipe. Olli moved her arm back just out of reach and pulled out her wallet with the other hand.

The cop's face darkened when he saw what she was holding. "Are you trying to buy me off?" he growled.

"No, of course not. You would never take it, like the good cop that you are. It's my badge. I carry it instead of wearing it." Olli tried another way to get the cop to loosen up about her being there. She glanced toward Dallas and noted that he was having some trouble with the security, too.

The less confident cops standing around them looked at her badge warily and backed away after she opened the wallet and the dim light from the overcast sky flashed off the surface. But the one cop that she had to worry about didn't move from in front of her.

He snatched it from her, his face still stormy.

"Where'd you get this?" he demanded. "Don't you know that it's against the law to impersonate an officer?" His tone was heated, and he finally managed to get a tight grip on her arm.

Olli recoiled back as far as his grip on her arm would allow. She was running out of patience, and he was holding her arm much tighter than he really needed to. She was about to inform him that his name might end up on the discharge list when Alan walked up.

Alan clapped a firm hand onto his shoulder, startling him a little. "That, my good Sir, is The District Detective you have by the arm. You can stop waving her badge in her face like that before she and I both lodge a complaint against you in your department." His eyes had a stern look in them.

Olli ripped her arm out of the cop's grip while he was distracted. Not hard, just enough to get out of his grip and catch his attention. She took her badge from him with another disarming smile. "Thank you." The wallet went directly back into her jacket pocket. "Nice to know that you're on your toes out here." Olli smiled at him again, with an edge, and walked a couple steps to where her father had just gotten Dallas out of an interrogation.

The three of them started down the block toward the bank.

"It seems that you're getting into a

lot of scrapes lately, Miss Olivia," Dallas observed, his eyes sparkling.

"That's not entirely true. That wasn't a scrape. I was going to get out of that," Olli disagreed slightly, taking note of the mirth in his eyes and not protesting too hard.

"Don't listen to her, Dallas. She's been telling me that since she could talk," Alan chuckled.

Olli looked at him, protest glinting in her eyes for a moment. That wasn't something that she wanted Dallas to know. It wasn't that her father was telling lies, or the entire truth, but her childhood scrapes were not something to discuss with Dallas of all people. Olli wasn't sure why, but it embarrassed her.

"Sorry about the hold-up. Most of these fine policemen are new to Big Town," Alan explained as they passed still more cops.

Olli shot a disapproving look toward two cops that walked past them and were leering in her direction. She narrowed her eyes and then looked at her father. "Are they fresh out of the academy?"

"No." Alan shook his head.

"Were they not informed that we don't wear our badges on our suit lapels around here?" Olli questioned, inching closer to Dallas when an older officer glowered at her. That threw her train of thought off its main track for a moment. Just twenty-four hours before she would have squared her shoulders and lift her chin at him so he knew that she wasn't afraid of his displeasure. Why did she suddenly feel she needed Dallas to protect her? She could take care of herself. It didn't make sense to Olli, but she had other, more important issues to figure out at the moment.

"If they're not from the academy, then where are they from, Sir?" Dallas asked, looking around at the stern-faced policemen who prowled about, making sure that stragglers who were missed at the front lines were sent back to the other side of the barricade.

"Eminences. They know all about organized crime. Unfortunately, they've run into so many fake ID's that they don't trust the real ones anymore. At least they take their job seriously," Alan informed, pulling his badge out and showing it to the two policeman standing guard on either side of the main doors to the bank.

They let him pass with a curt nod.

Olli and Dallas took the cue and flashed their badges at each of them and followed Alan into the bank's dim interior after receiving terse nods from the men.

Muted light came in through the big windows, and there wasn't a soul inside the main lobby of the bank. It looked like the bank had just been cleaned after years of being left empty. Olli didn't have much time to muse over the strange setting for very long. They had quickly crossed the spotless lobby and teller desks and came upon the vault.

Olli backed through the vault door when she heard the front door open and tipped an eyebrow at the man in blue who stepped into the lobby and stood at attention watching them. She quickly turned around and walked up to Alan. "Who called the watchdogs in?" the demand was light, but her eyes were not.

Alan sighed and shook his head slightly. "Mayor Anderson. His idea to barricade the entire block, too."

Mayor Anderson had only been mayor for about four months, but already he was starting to get on the Wainwrights' nerves. It wasn't that Alan didn't like him as a person; he just tended to over-react to some things. He insisted on handling things that the Wainwrights had handled since Big Town had been established. And when he took over like that, things were blown out of proportion--like policemen borrowed from Eminences and an entire block sealed off by the surly, suspicious cops.

Olli rolled her eyes. She disliked the mayor more than her father did. "Oh. How nice of him," She muttered. "So much for keeping the panic to a minimum." Olli rolled her eyes.

During the next ten minutes, the three of them searched the vault. It was completely empty. None of the drawers had a single penny in them, and there wasn't one carelessly dropped on the floor, either. All the drawers had their tags, and the metal fronts all were shiny enough to be almost reflective. The floor looked like it had recently been mopped and polished. And, much to their annoyance, none of the drawers looked like they had been opened at all.

Olli stopped once she got to about halfway into the vault. She studied the floor and drawers, searching for a missed detail, while Alan and Dallas continued deeper. Olli glared around the vault, expecting it to yield answers. It soon became a useless venture. "I don't understand it. How could this be possible? They swiped every bill and coin in the place, put all the drawers back and locked them. And it seems that they have a fetish for leaving nothing behind so they even played janitor and cleaned up behind themselves. No scuff marks, prints, dandruff. The money could have evaporated into thin air. Who does that?!" She started opening drawers with a handkerchief that she had pulled out of her inner pocket. "And besides that, the codes should have changed at least six different times while they cleaned this place out. How did the police not get a call?"

Alan sighed and shut his latest drawer with a little more force than was really necessary. "Apparently they found a way to shut the system down while they were here."

The three of them started toward the back doors of the bank, following the path the robbers took. If they had thought that the vault held no clues, it was nothing compared to the frustration that they felt when the shiny wood floors yielded no clues. The brass handrails had been polished and buffed to perfection. Olli, Dallas, and Alan brushed out through the back door onto the back steps leading into the alley, and frowned up at the sky. It had started raining while they were inside, and already things were starting to get wet.

Olli plunked down on the top step, ignoring the shower falling from above and the dampness seeping up from under her. She rubbed her temples. "We're sure they were here last night?" she wondered, frustration tainting her voice.

"Oh, they're quite real," Dallas assured, looking down at Olli.

Alan walked down the steps and surveyed the alley. "Very. They walked around the corner of the bank and bumped into a cop out on the beat."

Olli sighed. "But they didn't leave any evidence. Who's that good?" she demanded, looking first at Dallas, who was still standing over her on the top stair, and then at her father.

See What Happens Next!

Chapter 1

"The thing that has me confused is the fact that if they were good enough to slip in and out of this fine establishment twice without tippin' anythin' off…how were they careless enough to stumble over that cop who was out on the beat? Doesn't that seem just a little…" Dallas searched around for the right word, his right hand frozen in mid-air in the middle of a gesture. "Obviously staged…out of character…strange?" he offered, looking back and forth between the Wainwrights for their nods.

Olli thought about what he said. He did make a good point. She reached toward the handrail to pull herself up, but froze when Dallas' hand stopped her forward motion just before she touched it. Her eyes locked on his hand for a moment. She slowly looked back at him for the explanation and then jerked back around to look at the handrail as it dawned on her. *Of course. Why doesn't it surprise you that he thought of that first? Aces, Olli, he must think that you're the dumbest detective he's ever met! How did you not think of that?!* "Aces!"

A small smile spread across Alan's face and he nodded. He turned to the policeman who had been following them since they had walked into the bank, and his face instantly became professional "Go get the lab team; we might just have some fingerprints for them. Don't argue with me, Man! Go!" His normally pleasant tone took on a commanding quality.

It took a couple of minutes to scramble the lab team, so Olli, Dallas and Alan stepped under the overhang of the back door to keep from getting too wet while they waited. Alan had a pleased look on his face, Dallas was smirking to himself, and Olli was watching him out of the corner of her eye. She wasn't going to be caught off guard by the teasing remark that was sure to come. The lab team fortunately was able to get to the handrail in a decent time, and soon the three men were scouring the handrail for a clear fingerprint. Their search turned up two different sets of unidentified prints that didn't match up with any of the prints belonging to anyone who had, or did, work at the bank, or Ben Sandy himself.

After Olli managed to secure a copy of the prints for Lenny to look at, she and Dallas took their leave from Alan and the anthill-like activities that still surrounded the bank. There were other things that needed to happen that day.

They walked silently through a couple of back alleys, ignoring the pattering rain, both completely lost in their own thoughts. Olli was wondering if there were any connection between the men beating Dallas and the bank robbery. Dallas piecing together different pieces of the puzzle, trying not to get too distracted by the way Olli chewed on the inside of the left side of her bottom lip when she was thinking. Suddenly, a policeman a few years older than Dallas bumped into her and smiled apologetically. Olli really hadn't been paying that much attention to where she was walking, so she brushed it off and nodded good-naturedly...

Catch up with what Olli and Dallas do next in:

The Silence Broken: Part 2

Coming Soon!

ABOUT THE AUTHOR

Janelle Arens grew up loving Nancy Drew and the Hardy Boys mysteries, but the intrigue of hidden rooms and trap doors and staircases did not dwindle as she grew older. Dick Tracy became a new favorite. Then one day, her best friend discovered a distant family tie to the James Younger Gang, and a different adventure, a historical one, began. From the outlaw bands from the Wild West to the tales of famous Mob bosses was just a short trek. Her interest in the Prohibition Era events led her to a lot of reading. Her writing skills advanced as well. Janelle became a mischievously clever writer who pulls the reader into her books with ease, delivering adventure and plot twists with a generous dose of humor.

Janelle lives in southwest Michigan with her husband, James, and no dog...yet.

Made in the USA
Lexington, KY
25 July 2017